STORY

OF A

TALE-MAKER

by

FRANCIS

VOIGNIER

Cover design by Francis Voignier
Photo source: artisteer/iStock

Edited by Bruce Malamut

This book is a work of fiction. Any relation to living individuals, at the exception of public figures whose names are respectfully used in the context of their professions, businesses, and/or social influence, is purely coincidental.

Library of Congress Cataloging-in-Publication Data
Voignier, Francis 1954—United States
Story of a Tale-Maker/Francis Voignier
ISBN-13: 978-1-73455-519-6
ISBN-10: 1-73455-519-X

Fiction – Mystery – Metaphysics – Philosophy

francisvoignier.com
Dolosse & Writs, Eureka CA, USA

LIST OF CONTENTS

My deepest thanks and appreciation go to
my life partner, Rev. Elisabeth Zenker,
for her invaluable trust and support.

NOTE FROM THE AUTHOR

My editor, dear friend, and writer extraordinaire, Bruce Malamut, suggested in a recent email that the very act of writing from the standpoint of a fully fleshed-out character such as the one in this book was bound to blow up in my face. His exact words: "The problem with transposing the acting device of the 4th Wall into our medium is that – by the very fact of writing with its resulting 'trails' or 'evidence' the transposition invariably blows the subtlety of the former acting stunt out of the water exposing the con to our audience so loud and clear."

I concurred.

Along that line of thought, one must understand that "Tale" is a story for the sake of a story, written by me, and obviously not the character – as much as I would love for the substitution to charm the reader by placing her/him center-front.

Any attempt by me to disclaim taking said reader into my personal rabbit hole would be futile. Obviously the message is mine. But we're talking about a tale, which forbids me to prevent anyone from choosing their own way to interpret it. The one thing that resonates here is that fiction exists for the sake of entertainment, while I hope it does its part in contributing to the larger picture as well. In the end, and based on myriad personal traits and preferences, the reader either relates or not.

And Bob's your uncle!

~Francis Voignier~

1 – THE LINE ACROSS

I am not the author. The author exists across the line, in a world which, in subtle ways, is different from mine. My name is Janette. The author's name is somewhere on the cover, or in the film credits. It is my choice to remain discreet about identities.

The assumption is that characters such as me are often confused with the product of the imaginative. Somewhere in the unruly world of potential are we to rise, come to form, and be herded along the thorny trails of loose drafts, then propelled across stories as they gain momentum, only to get old or suffer premature deaths, or worse even—exist forever in the layers of uncertainty. All of it couldn't be further removed from the truth.

My world and I were around long before the "now" of these very pages, and thus, we shall continue on with our journey, well beyond the parting credits.

To cut to the chase, I am the one who connected with the writer via the maze of corridors that separates our respective realities. I chose my "character," so to speak, one whose curiosity has been, for a long time, the subject of my own. He is of course aware, although unsure, that something is going on. While he is willing to accept the concept of traditional channeling via the good auspices of the muse of inspiration, he is reluctant to let go of the element of proprietorship. I can't really blame him, for his world is not designed to stray from the base on which it stands; at least for now.

So, the line in question, though not physically crossable in either direction, but awareness being what it is, allows in fact for a certain level of exchange, even if only one party fully gets the gist of it. From the author's standpoint, I shall only remain an amenable mental cutout. I am used to it.

As to me, I'm only glad to have been able to connect. That, in of itself, is what I have been living for, or more precisely, what all of us in my trade are striving for.

— o —

Yesterday, my friend John came to visit in his brand new auto. He's very proud of the fact perpetual motion is no longer out of the reach of the consumer. Me, I'm not so much into technology, though I appreciate a smart invention when put to good use.

The night before, John had dreamt he was a cartoon character, which had left him unsettled. He wanted to share in hopes of dissipating the sickening feeling in his guts combined with the awkwardness in his mind. Plus, it prevented him from enjoying his new toy. Not that John is shallow, but he does like his machines. We agreed it would pass. You see, we don't do cartoons, no matter what. Perhaps there exists a far-remote, perverse corner of existence in which characters spend their entire lives bashing each other, but I don't fathom much purpose to it. As far as I am concerned, those will strictly remain the byproducts of the imaginary.

We don't live very far apart, John and I; barely separated, we are, by a stretch of road between two bodies of water connecting our two towns, mine being the biggest one—practically a city—by the name of Bayville; John's is Junction Station, ten kilometres to the north.

2

We try to connect once a week to chat over dinner at one of the seafood places along the port. John's working with an action writer, and of course, fast autos and ample gadgetry prevail. OK, so I've let the cat out: we don't just tell our stories; in most instances, we adapt them to the basic profile of the "character" at the time of conception. It doesn't mean that we never tell it like it is; I am the living proof of it. My author gets his served straight up. In recap, John and I compare notes, along with helping each other with connectivity, which requires the utmost in skills.

While, for the moment, my "character" appears disposed-enough to embrace the process, John, on the other hand, is having trouble with his assignment. Not all writers are made the same, and in John's case, promises of a strong "collaboration" are being tested. It was a sure thing, a mature and skillful wordsmith, but just like that, bam—a breakdown! John says he wants out, but the Governor has the last say. The fundamental issue with (let's call him Case X,) lies in his obstinacy to control the "flow," meaning that, essentially, the data cannot go through without coming out all wrong. Simply, if John fails at rectifying the lack of traction, "X" will end up with a lousy book and John with an incontrovertible sense of doom. That could explain the cartoon nightmare. I wish I could help by tapping his line, but I am not permitted; plus, I'm already taken.

We normally order the fish since it's a fish place, but John goes for pork, knowing all too well that pork is imported from China, expensive, and fresh-frozen— which translates as sometimes frozen/sometimes not-so- much. It all depends on the age of the ship that brings it over. Long story short, it's out of character for John to splurge on a bad cut of meat. I sense mounting self-loathing; hence all the better reasons why I should help.

— o —

Case X is a classic example of someone overtaken by his own worst enemy, notably—the self. It's a common occurrence on that side of the line. John will have to take a step back in order to sort things out. Right now, he has become entangled with the "character" to the point of practically being reduced to a part in a bad script. It's called a "swap." It happens a lot with novices, thus the proliferation of books of no consequence, but in John's case, it is a rarity. A swap, as much as it can be endearing in the young, is a tragedy among the mature "tale-makers." It means you've lost your touch. And John knows what it entices as far as the Governor is concerned.

I bring the pork to his attention, enquiring about his reason for the order. He looks at me with a blank stare, as if suddenly finding himself in a scene of unfamiliar settings. He calls the garçon and switches for the cod.

— o —

So far, so good; I don't think I presently need to worry about my "character." He's just going through the motions, only pausing for minor corrections here and there—nothing fundamental. After the fish, John and I walk along the boardwalk on our way to the Ferris wheel. We enjoy watching people being people; especially when the air is filled with laughter and lovers kiss freely on the benches lining our path, although tonight the fog has

4

rolled into town with a full palette of grays. Bayville has its moods, which often reflects those of the souls of its inhabitants.

John and I are not an item, though we've been friends like forever. We grew up in Junction Station amid the vestiges of the long Summer of Love. It seemed, at the time, that the big cities had emptied their reserves of non-conformists into the small communities of the north, colourful people with dreams like fat puffy clouds and smiles for miles. We ran among them, two kids in a playground filled with moving props, the pungent smoke of incense and skunk weed filling our heads with fantasy. Things are very different now. Seasons steadily lay awash the shores of history to prepare them for the latest in evo-trends. We are presently, and short of a better description, in between decors.

By the time the no-longer gleaming surf of love had covered our beaches with its last layer of froth, John and I had parted to follow the call of our inner voices. Mine insisted I saw the world, so my parents obliged by sending me abroad among the French, while John's had him study creative writing in the huge eastern cities, across the boundaries of the range. It took years before we reconnected. We actually ran into each other two decades ago in downtown Bayville while queuing at a restaurant. We spent nearly twenty minutes chatting before linkage. That was how much we had changed, not just physically, but identity-wise.

But it's only lately that we've made the habit of meeting once a week over fish, which synchs with John's breakup from a long affair of the heart. He swears that our ritual isn't to compensate for that loss. I feel no sexual attraction between us and I'm reassured he intends on respecting that space. That distance is what actually keeps us close—a play of opposites that satisfies me immensely.

But lately, with the unscheduled struggle in his life, a veering of sort has left marks in the sand. I have always been of the belief that we exist on the precarious balance of giving and receiving, wherein by maintaining a foot in each camp, we stand at the fulcrum point of owning our full senses. John's personal tipping of the scales is gently tugging at my shields, as if to persuade me that it is alright to let one foot slip towards the force. I don't buy it, and I'm sure he isn't conscious of it. It doesn't seem like much, but the order of pork has left me on edge. For the first time, I am aware our relationship might pose a minor challenge. Meanwhile, the present needs me whole. I'm at odds with my promise to help and my reluctance to deliver. My integrity relies on my ability to juggle the two without losing the axis of symmetry. But I haven't promised anything to John; I just said I would try to help. The promise is a personal one; I shall decide later as to its fate.

——— o ———

2 – FRANCE

Interesting that the "character" should be French. Actually, in his case, it's hard to tell. But I digress—it's just a happy parallel. As I said, I landed in France. I traveled by boat, a two-week voyage that enrobed my experience in delicious mystique. I didn't really know what to expect, save for what we were told via the channels of the rarely verified, which as it turned out was worse than one could imagine. For one thing, nobody wears berets. For two, hardly anyone smokes anymore, not since the hard campaign that has instilled an indubitable sense of impending doom in the heart of every Gaul and non-Gaul alike. What did it was hidden in the syntax—an audible implant. It was a one-time deal, a brief amendment to an otherwise immutable law. What was also different from the uneducated propaganda about the French was the fact that they actually are nice people with no issue using their rudimental English to help the lost and clueless. No, they don't hate "les americains"!

I disembarked in Le Havres, a wide-eyed teen with her hair blown in all directions from the restless sea winds. I was liberated from the inner prison of partial ignorance, free to roam the uncharted with careless nonchalance. I was one of the lucky ones, I heard, but I never let that outside projection touch me. Luck isn't part of my vernacular when it comes to hard-earned chips. I owned that trip as my one calling, a choice that belonged to the sacred.

I was met on the quay by Chantal, who would become my good friend for the months to come. She was a gorgeous red hair, slightly round in the hips, with a smile that could melt a heart on the spot. I adored her from that very moment. Chantal was in charge of helping me navigate the labyrinthine system of the French. She had been assigned to me by the organization responsible for coordinating traffic between sister colleges. All went flawlessly under the watch of deft Chantal, though to be fair to myself, I wasn't totally resourceless. And so, after a short stay in Le Havres, we boarded a train to Paris— one of the steampunk rapid transports still very much in vogue these days. It felt like we sat immobile while the countryside flew by us in a blur of green punctuated by the intermittent rust of village roofs. The effect was one that stimulated the senses in orgasmic waves. Chantal reveled in the reaction of my "first time," by simply looking into my eyes with a complicit twinkle.

We were served light fares and drinks from ambulant carts pushed by garçons trimmed and emblazoned in the trademark colours of the Railroads of France. But if the appearances gave out an air of stuffy demeanour, humour prevailed via the appropriate jest of words, the perfectly timed wink, or the suggestive twitch of sensuous lips. I soaked it all up!

Paris was a blast! I had never been in such a vast city; never mind the fact it was also very old. We swam in wrought iron, zinc roofs, cobblestones, limestone, marble, and the ubiquitous copper that gleamed from all corners, regardless of where we gazed. People poured into the streets from every alley, store, café/bar, train station, cinema, and museum to join in the general cacophony of old, rattling hydro-motors; raspy horns; sidewalk barkers; and drunken poets. I declared, there and then, that I was in love, vanquished by the inebriating power of France's spell. It amused Chantal to see me in such a state of elation, just as it amuses me now to reflect on that part of my past. I adore that child!

— o —

We stayed in le Quartier Latin for a week, a place buzzing with international students and leftists, where young mustached men playacted life in grand, refined gestures, while their "gypsied-out" dames danced in circles, their light, colourful skirts whirling in the sun, revealing the beauty of their curvaceous forms. Life was a stage, with every fountain a prop inviting an act of spontaneity. I wasn't one to just stand by and watch. I danced and laughed with them. Chantal, in all her bubbliness, was the shyer of the two—Eastern French reserve, as she called it. I could go on and on about Paris, but there was more to France to be seen. Soon, we were on another train, onwards to connect with Straßburg where I would be studying for a degree in world diplomacy during the course the following three years.

— o —

There is much to say about Straßburg and the people who popped in and out of my life, as I busied myself with studies. The mix of modern and gothic architecture was to my taste, particularly the old colombage buildings with their pots of geraniums at every window. I am glad craftsfolks were putting the last touches to the cathedral's second tower while I lived there. I got drunk at the post-completion ceremony and had sex with Kurt. Not my best behaviour considering I didn't really like beer and couldn't care less for Kurt by then. At least I didn't get pregnant. So yes, my time in the city was occasionally punctuated by the odd digression, but apart from that, I operated solo with weekly rituals at one of the film houses. In retrospect, Straßburg had a sobering effect on my person, in the sense that all which had stimulated me during my short stay in Paris was gone within months of setting foot in the eastern city. It was OK with Chantal by my side, but after she left for England, following that first brutal winter, I lost the impetus to go beyond the motions. In all fairness, the place had nothing to do with my emotional state—I was simply missing Bayville, unwilling to admit it to myself.

—o—

My emotions didn't make Straßburg; they slightly watered down its colours at best. I wasn't depressed per se; I actually enjoyed the vortex-like quality that lived in the lower region of my belly. As one knows, the city is made of two parts—West-Straßburg on the French side of the Rhine, and East-Straßburg in Germania. Even though France was my place of residence, I bore the weight of the historical duality that defines the region. Most natives to the west still speak German or a version of it, while across the waters, French is only sporadically used. My parents had thought that by sending me there, I had a better chance of assimilating multiple cultures. They were right on that account, but I never felt as one with any of them while in Straßburg. I am guilty of painting the place in tones of melancholia, and as I already said—perhaps unfairly. I cannot fully disengage from the "character" at the end of the connection; oftentimes it requires a form of concession on our parts, "tale-makers," to help the flow. That being said, my experience in Straßburg was far from *triste*. The vortex I spoke of earlier was my own though. The quality of being a fish out of water had caught up with me—the novelty had lost its sheen.

— o —

The first two months that took us, Chantal and I, to the steps of winter, were purely magical. We laughed, we sang, we hugged, and I have to admit, we slept together. It would never have occurred to us that we could have been lovers, so natural was the setting, but in perspective, we were. One may say that innocence is the perfect shield against having to define experience and the self. We walked hand in hand like natives amid the stone peepers, in the cross-flashing of their memory boxes. We were the mysterious blur at the corner of a photograph, the rarely noticed strangers in the background of a shaky video—we were the spirits that rode the winds of unseen corridors. We met Kurt and Peter on one such walk. They came to us, slightly inebriated, with the false confidence of those too sure of themselves, but we found them endearing all the same. Their faces were red from laughter and the premature seasonal cold. Neither of them was exceptionally good looking, or sufficiently tall by most standards, but they both had a twinkle in their eyes. Enough said! That night, we all went to a cinema to watch a couple of classic French noirs. The boys tried to flirt with us, but we had the upper hand. Eventually, they quieted down. Later, we went out for drinks, but Chantal and I called it quit before mistakes were made. Peter and Kurt walked out unsteadily into the night with our phone numbers. Somewhere, in the back of our minds, we wished they quickly forgot about us. It didn't happen.

— o —

My studies were doing well. I loved my classes, my grades were top, and I knew I would excel in the field. World diplomacy is a special branch of political science. Precisely, it is P.S. on steroids. The point is to understand the importance of the cultural backgrounds at the base of foreign communication. It seems simple in principal, until you have to immerse yourself in it. Then it's like navigating a Turkish bazaar in Chinatown, except trickier.

— o —

After Chantal and, oddly, Peter left for London, I experienced a void. My heart was broken in slow motion, while betrayal laid its mat of numbness, as if to ironically cushion the fall of its pieces. Let's face it, the surprise was expected, as Chantal had by then deserted the warmth of our bed for a room with Peter, during which time I saw more of Kurt than I wished to. So, in an act of quasi-bravery, I stubbornly buried myself in studies. It was also a good way to keep Kurt out of my sight, though he wasn't necessarily collaborating. He came drunk to my door on many an occasion, begging on his knees for me to let him in. I didn't budge. The drama morphed into love declarations, which I also turned down; then came the stormy weather. Getting drunk and having sex with him was my one moment of weakness, but it was also me trying to get it over with. The very next morning, I asked him to leave and never return. I must have misjudged the

12

power of my words, but the fact is I never saw him again.

I returned to my studies all the more resolute, with results far exceeding my expectations, as well as those of my professors. Towards the end of my second year, I was asked into the dean's office, where a tall gentleman of good manners I had never seen before, greeted me. He convinced me to follow him into an adjacent room accessed via a swinging bookcase, meticulously closing behind us, while looking around the space as if to make sure it wasn't bugged. He brought a chair to the front of the desk, asking me to please sit down.

I was certain I had slipped into an alternate reality rife with the intrigue of soirées noires. I made a mental note of easing off the film houses. But this wasn't an illusion brought on by a lapse in sanity; the man was real and quite pleasant, which made for balancing out some of the apprehension. I don't recollect ever hearing his name—I certainly didn't feel at liberty to ask. But he did mention mine—Janette Trudy Smyth, from the North-western Territory of the Amerikas. By then, my French, German, and Italian had been granted native level status, so it was a rather odd choice for him to opt for English when it was only spoken in special classes. He assured me the reason was to establish a sense of confidentiality—it was no longer about studies, though they had brought me there.

The gentleman proposed that I enroll in a custom program for the rest of my stay in Straßburg, promising the terms of my graduation would remain unaffected. As far as he was concerned, I knew as much as the school was able to teach me, just from the fact that I was a natural. By contrast, my new studies would propel me into the realm of specialists in cross-cultural communication. I was far from probing the depths of what he meant by that, but I stood at the stage at which a worthy challenge was welcome; thus, I accepted.

— o —

The two-month-long summer break afforded me my first visit to Junction Station since my departure. Things had changed, or rather, I had. What I had missed was no longer there. Instead I yenned for my home back in France. It worried me that quiet forbearance had overtaken the flamboyance that had accompanied me into the unknown. I felt the early stages of adulthood were stifling something precious in me, snuffing the joy of my youth to replace it with the quality of cold steel. I wasn't ready to completely surrender to the metamorphosis. I wanted to be back on the docks of Le Havre where Chantal took my hand for the first time. It was there that I belonged. I yearned for the magical train rides with their cart-pushing garçons high on charm, for the mischievous tease of copper glow and steam gauges, and for the world of thin, mustached lads and their Gypsy goddesses dancing around fountains in the golden and mystifying late afternoons of le Quartier Latin.

I thought of transferring to Paris to finish my master there, but only the University of Straßburg offered that course. I was teetering on the edge of confusion. How could I call my home a place I didn't want to be in? Something was seriously wrong with me. In fact, my true home was in between the old and the new, the median point that demarcated two selves at odds with each other. One had birthed fantasy; the other was killing it. Only in the middle could it thrive and feed my soul.

So, I took advantage of my time in Bayland County to reacquaint myself with the previous me. Of course, I would never be her again, but if I could extract the qualities I deemed necessary to my sanity, I would thank that child forever for her cooperation. By the end of my stay, I was back on track, free of the dullness that had whitewashed my true colours. I readied myself for Straßburg with a new outlook at my prospects. I wasn't going to let Rhine Melancholia sweep me under her murky waters, or an alluring, secret side-program sway me off-course. I was the one who would set the tone!

It was a good thing what I did with my head back in Junction Station—it was the only thing—the last of the auspicious times for saving a young heart from drifting into forgetfulness. It served me well.

— o —

Straßburg immediately changed. For one thing, the geraniums discoursed at great length on the topic of fair weather from their high perches. The new cathedral bell rang in joyful punches chased by myriad elfin overtones. But mostly, the city lifted my heart in double armloads of hope. I called it Neu-Straßburg, for it was just that—new, or reborn. The great surprise came with my introduction to the program. I only saw the tall gentleman once again during that time, as he welcomed me upon my return to brief me over the necessary instructions to the enrollment process, though it is to be said that his influence would be greatly felt further down the line. Then he was gone. The surprise in question was in the people I met there, a wonderful and colourful group of fast-thinking huggers, who showed no reserve in touching me, running their fingers through my hair, seemingly testing suppleness, while introducing me to the mechanics that would determine the course of my final year on campus. I felt immediately at home in the sense that my qualities were being absorbed by an understanding kinship. It was the in-between zone I had envisioned in my daydreaming, back in Bayland County. It didn't quite occur to me that I was a late admission, joining a class in its second year, but by the time I learned about it, it was no longer of consequence.

— o —

The building I was to move my things to, and wherein I would attend all of my classes, was at the far end of campus, overlooking the Rhine, a large four story red sandstone structure, three hundred years of age. The curved grand staircase gave the illusion of having been carved from a single piece. Instead of the coldness associated with stone, its wide railing, by contrast, felt warm to the touch, almost as if radiating in synchrony with the caress of the hand to match the body's temperature. It was a very welcoming sensation with a promise of safety. It also suggested there wasn't much of a reason to venture beyond those walls. It was a self-contained organism with its own kitchens, library, and gymnasiums; with the added bonus of being totally hidden by ancient trees from the rest of campus, while it offered its own exit into town—a world within a world I never knew existed in my two years having studied there. My room was on the top floor, at the end of a long corridor. The small cut-glass window opened on a grassy field that followed the

Rhine till it came to a halt at the base of a bank-retaining stone wall. I loved the view, alive with the river's slow flowing waters—it felt like time moving.

— o —

It didn't take long for me to understand that the program strayed substantially from World Diplomacy, yet it purported to support a greater form of it. We were introduced incrementally to the notion that a world in need of our help existed beyond the conventional one; help to come in the form of information conveyed across yet-to-be-defined thresholds. The program would teach us how to identify those boundaries and connect with the individuals at the receiving end of the "experiment," for it was exactly that—an experiment.

My co-students and I amounted to a grand total of eighteen. There were three professors in charge, two males and a female, answering to the mysterious tall gentleman who, as I recently learned, was referred to as the Governor. His regular absences, it was said, accounted for his travels to faraway places, for the purpose of gathering knowledge. A good half of us were skeptical believers, but we had no valid reason to seek to dislodge the accuracy of that statement.

It was also said that the Governor was the founder of the Program, (a word I shall, from now on, capitalize,) but determining the date of its inception was difficult, especially since the professors were surprisingly vague about it. The information on how these three individuals came to be the teachers of such a well-kept secret was restricted. It seemed that the courses, as new as they were, dabbed at some form of ancient science, as it was whispered in the halls during recess. There was surely a beginning that rooted in the loamy underbrush of fallow fields. Or was it a lone weed among the wheat? There were many questions that preceded my steps during the first few weeks, but they steadily became part of the daily ritual, to inconspicuously vanish from the front desk of reasoning. There were no direct answers to a conglomerate unknown fed by tributaries of unreachable headwaters. I was a young sponge eager to absorb, bent on instilling a dash of the dramatic within my wimpy assumptions. Of course, the Program was borne of the common knowledge of olden eras, a tender jut that came as a reminder of purpose for those with "special aptitudes," as we were briefed. We hadn't unwittingly been lured into a sect, only that the Program required the room to breath away from the brouhaha of campus. The building had only, until recently, been used for the storage of relics, archives, and other dust collectors. The Governor, with the help of private financiers, was able to acquire the space and its surroundings to make them the Program's own, providing they remained integral to the university. In a unique clause, it was specified that its main aim was to serve as an overflow, meaning that there was no such thing as the Program until extraordinary students were introduced to it.

Of course, it was a shocker to be associated with such distinction. I worked hard for my grades, but I never thought I had special attributes deserving of the consideration. I simply said yes to an offer, never really putting much thought into why I ended up in the dean's office in the first place. As it turned out, my passion for understanding balanced communication amid adverse settings was what made me stick out. I was not merely learning for a degree, I had given myself to it, so that it would become me. But then again, I never truly reflected on the nuance; I was magnetized by it as much as I drew it to me, like lovers brought together by the pull of silent contracts in the form of suitably coded hormones. I was called to duty by innate curiosity, by the thirst to fill the void issued to the offspring of distinct, yet embryonic choices; an offspring that would, one day, become the future me.

Our abilities, as students, came to light in spontaneous outbursts. Friendly tensions built until release. We learned to meditate our way along private channels, towards the promised thresholds. We came to hubs of countless options to furthering our explorations; each of us employing unique pathways. But the methodology was universal, which inherently consisted of teaching us how to navigate the deeper strata of the self, and to recognize its significant markers. Each stepping stone was determined by how much further consciousness had traveled, and by what instance of communication it had vitalized within that environment. For example, in my last "outing," I was met by an "aspect personality" that complimented me on my journey, thanking me for having confirmed what they had all along suspected would manifest. In other words, I had bumped into another traveler. My luck was that it was a mutually beneficial encounter—we were both aware! We met on a few more occasions after that.

I could go on and on about the early steps of the Program, but I don't see the point. I wish not to preach, while I detest having to explain why I love what I do, to ears with short reception skills. In the end, it amounts to reaching willing souls, whether they know it or not, in places where our talents can potentially be appreciated.

We are artistes, artistes with a deep calling for helping other artistes in associated settings. I am a "tale-maker," a communication expert, and in his world, my "character" is recognized as a writer. In what summed up to be an outlandish concept at the time; we cannot successfully operate without each other.

And so, my last year in France turned out to be one of the best I ever had. The Program was a perfect fit, while all around me, life had expanded in leaps of immeasurable spans. I can truly say that birds sang truer, colours bounced livelier, and people loved better. Talking of love, I adored everyone, including the professors, and my sex life evolved exponentially. If blitheness had brought me to France, a firm sense of belonging teamed to high-spiritedness was seen accompanying me on the ship platform out of Le Havre. The ghost of Chantal was nowhere to be seen—I thanked her for it.

—— o ——

3 – MONTEREY

Back in Junction Station, I opted to immerse myself in simple tasks before reconnecting with the Program. I helped my dad with fixing the old barn, and my mom, tending to the garden. I figured I deserved to let my mind rest, while the dreams of my sleeping self took care of putting order to the clutter. My renewed acquaintance with familiar objects brought me to the door of memories of my youth with John. Where was he? I hadn't heard of his whereabouts since he drifted from my line of sight. I was told he had been in town before taking off again, so I deemed that a visit with his mother was in order. John had been accepted at Emory University in East Amerika to study creative writing, and where he graduated with honours. But his return to Bayland County found him a changed young man, with a predisposition to keep his distance from probing, and in a state of quasi-emotional privation. He left without as much as telling where he was destined to. His mother took the slight with brave stoicism, simply raising her shoulders in who-knows-what's-up-with-him resignation. I guessed college had had an adverse effect on his nature, turning the sweet to sour in only three years. Broken promises could have been a factor, but personal dreams only held personal promises. Unless, of course, there were other reasons, and as it turned out, there were. But later on that!

A few of us, students, were to connect with a West Amerikan Chapter of the Program, a schedule that was only made available after the final exam. It could have been a surprise to learn there was more than met the eye, but we had become immune to last minute disclosures through our training. We, by nature, had been exposed to all flavours of revelation via the spelunking of the deep self. The school was situated near the San Carlos Cathedral in Monterey, a place I had visited more than once in my teens as part of the summer rituals of traveling the Pacific coast with my bohemian parents. I was rejoiced by not having to be uprooted and replanted across the globe. Monterey was my kind of town, a manageable long drive straight down from Bayville. And since I had inherited my dad's vintage hydro-powered automobile—I was officially set for a new adventure.

— o —

Monterey's another bay town, so there was geographical kinship right out of the bag. But unlike the long deserted beaches of Bayland, the coast there was packed with structures, some of them overlooking the surf. By comparison, my natal Pacific appeared less behaved, where those buildings would have stood no chance of not being somewhat roughed up. Maybe we shouldn't have called it the Pacific in my parts, although I cannot think of a less kind name for it.

Six students from Straßburg joined me for the advanced course. Although the building did not provide lodging, it had an adequately supplied cafeteria, free of charge. I shared a cottage with Chloe, near the water, which afforded us quick access to Del Monte Beach for our early morning barefoot walks.

I prefer to keep the professor's name confidential for reasons both personal and beyond my control. He was a flamboyant man in his late thirties whose depth of knowledge was so bottomless, that his genius radiated through his being in a big golden aura—the biggest I had been allowed to see so far. Talking of auras, it was part of the course in Straßburg to refine the ability to read spectral emissions. Most people are generally careless about shielding themselves, but for those with the knowledge, the aura can be made visible or not. It was, and of course still is, an issue of trust in our environment. The Program required that no-one was to shield under any circumstance in class; trust being paramount to authenticity, a quality at the base of inner strength. We had to learn to become so transparent that energy could only flow through us, in rhythm with the beat of the heart—a metaphor I came to dearly love. The Professor, as I shall call him from now on, taught us how to identify kindred souls across the line and latch onto their energy with the equivalent of a living contract. Depending on the reality behind them, these entities responded with a range of awareness that varied from clear to nonexistent, yet there would not have been any contract if there hadn't existed a form of agreeability at some level. Consciousness is a funny business for those who choose not to heed its language. Why some societies have opted to operate in the dark is beyond my comprehension, but even our kind isn't immune to darkness; hence the reason for the Program.

Nurturing a connection takes time and ample patience. For example, the present "character" was made aware to me a few years after Monterey, but it took forever to "coerce" him into developing his writing skills, which I am still working on. On the other hand, I was rewarded by his propensity for listening to inner voices. Hopefully, one day, we'll meet one on one. That's the goal at my end! In the meantime, much was to be picked in the no-longer fallow gardens of my soul—what to do with the harvest was next on the agenda.

I came across many inner travelers on my journeys, who like the first one, were more into validating their theories than interested in sharing rides. We had to find those with the collaborating spirit, as well as the need to heal their worlds. Generally speaking, it involved souls who had the mental agility to recognize their limitations, while willing to take chances crossing them. This may sound relatively simple conceptually, but believe me, when you know these people are not aware they're looking for something, in places they have no idea how to recognize, it takes a complex, strategic approach to get their attention. But when you do, they generally open themselves to receptivity. You see, we can't look into their worlds with their eyes, anymore than we can with ours; we are only capable to meet at the border. From that point on, the information gets hauled via the intuitive channels to both the intellectual and emotional chambers, but only after inspection by the "belief system police." In other words, from the threshold on, it's out of our hands. We can only hope that the work gets done. Of course, we have acquired the means to read the messenger's auratic field—that was one of the major courses at the Monterey Chapter. I might be getting over my head with the descriptive, for I'm not so good at laying out the technical details of my work. Let's just say that with practice, both parties develop a heart connection that allows for a merging of consciousness. Because of that connection, we can recognize when there is obstruction at the receiving end. Then comes the time when finesse is most required. I shall make myself clearer as we go.

Monterey gave us the tools necessary to establish contact, but it came with ample servings of frustration and humility. It wasn't a totally joyless process though; eventually, we stopped losing sleep over our failed attempts. The Professor was always there to reassure us of the normality of small steps. We had first to accept that in order to leave the space of the theoretical, logic too had to stay behind. That was not always obvious!

— o —

The remaining eleven students out of Straßburg ended up, as we soon learned, joining two other Chapters, the Moscow and Osaka ones. The Professor also mentioned the plans for a new branch in Rio de Janeiro, but it was yet to be determined who would teach the class, since there were only six qualifying members. News from France informed us that twenty fresh students had been selected for the Program by the Governor. I didn't know it then, but it turned out that John was one of them.

— o —

I loved Monterey, and since I was able to visit my parents regularly, I never felt a sense of not belonging. The Pacific Coast was a big home. Besides Chloe, my social group included the Professor and two of his friends, Alice and Max, both freelance journalists for the Herald and the Sentinel. Of course, the other students showed up frequently at the cottage for food, games, and whatever students do when they shake loose. In fact, we ended up at each other's places on a rotating basis. Besides Max and Alice, we rarely accepted outsiders into our circle.

25

We admitted to being cliquey, but it was more by code than from superciliousness, for we never looked down on anyone—to the contrary. For reasons pertinent to my kind, I was not sexually interested in men my age, or women for that matter, though I was at a stage at which men made for the larger portion of my activities. I slept with the Professor at least once a week, and was in a love triangle with Alice and Max with equal regularity. I enjoyed pleasing the body, mine and theirs. I knew some of the boys in the group wished to seduce me, but they were wise enough to heed the auratic code. I loved them like brothers and sisters, but not like men and women of substance. And that—in the eye of the Professor—was what set me apart. By the end of the semester, with high grades, an aced test, and precious new knowledge teamed with applied abilities under my wing, I was asked to partake in the opening of the Rio de Janeiro Chapter planned a year down the line, and urged to enroll in the Master Course, with the aim of joining as the seventh scholar to teach the Program. It was an honour beyond my wildest expectations. I didn't bother thinking about it; I said yes on the spot! On the only downside, I was going to be far away from home for the longest time, for it required my return to Straßburg for a year, before traveling to South Amerika. On the upside, the Governor was to privately tutor me.

—— o ——

4 – THE GOVERNOR

Upon my arrival in Straßburg, I went directly to campus. My France phase was over, for the magic that spread before me was in the form of an exploding passion for my studies and future work. It didn't mean that my feet were no longer touching the ground, but the material in most of its manifestations was failing to summon my interest. Gone were the film houses, the architecture, and the cathedral bells. The human achievement had lost its place to more humble attractions, such as the natural order and life connections. I was slowly learning to become one with all, without the need to understand why. Trust and love had freed me from the shackles of doubt, and in the process, brought me to the gates of a spiritual reality few come to acknowledge during their human travels. Forget religions, or even pagan gatherings, for they only purvey to false interpretations. I shall leave faith untouched, as I trust it caters to greater truths, so don't slay me quite yet!

The Governor wasn't there to welcome me back. I heard he had been away for the entire year, and no-one knew where "away" was. I was beyond evaluating the merit of the slight discomfort that accompanied what I took for a remark about his absence. If the faculty felt somewhat diminished by not having been kept in the know of the Governor's whereabouts, it certainly wasn't aware of it. I brushed that revelation away with a quick thought about my arrangements, and proceeded towards registering for class. I was assigned the same room. For a brief instant, I cogitated on the odds, but I was intuitively assured that it had been planned that way. It was a gift of respect towards those who had left their indelible mark on the Program—mine being one of total commitment to it.

The week that followed was mostly taken with summarizing the steps of my personal evolution since the commencement of the Program. I wasn't taking notes per se, not even mental ones; simply, I wanted to relive the whole of it in "multi-motion." By that, I mean aligning my various phases side by side, as opposed to un-reeling a continuous ribbon. It's a form of time management for the thinking process. It was all clear to me; my calling had not lied. I had been drawn to the Program by immutable forces which I recognized as of my own making. No, I do not intend to imply that such choices were made during my youth; I was too busy being a child then, but rather, within an ambiance that exists outside of time. Please, allow yourselves to imagine there is such a place! The Program is akin to a living organism that gains in vitality as one learns to acknowledge the reasons for its existence. As it becomes you, it expands to make room for others to join. One may say that it is a gestaltic entity composed of members of the student body, but that would suggest that we don't have mobility of our own. It is in fact quite the contrary, since mobility, instead of being impaired, grows exponentially, not only in speed, but also in breadth of territory. But back to Straßburg!

Beside the recap of my past two years in the Program, I prepared for my meeting with the Governor. There wasn't much to prepare for on the surface, since I had no idea what was on his mind, or even when he would be back, but I immediately put myself wholly in the space of the one I intended to become. I had, of course, paid close attention to the methodology used by my predecessors and I noticed there always was a personal touch to it, an interpretation that gave girth to the subject. It was important, in that it made me realize how rigidity was not going to work. The only discipline that applied was showing up on time; the rest was improvisation on a theme. Essentially, the students I would end up teaching were also the ones who would make me evaluate my own process, which I loosely refer to as "circular knowledge." But when the Governor failed to show up for the second week in a row, I took matters a step further by setting camp in the allotted classroom, and teaching myself from the podium, pretending I was at the desk below. I used the "ribbonized" version of my education as chapters in the course, pitting them against each other in mind and soul, with the aim of enriching the topic at hand, namely, how to go forward. Had anyone ventured into the room during my off-the-wall sessions, I do not doubt I would have become the topic of much speculation. But the space was off-limit to all, since I had been put in charge of resetting the entry code.

After a while, I began to think that my tutor had no intention of being present. If he had guessed I would be teaching myself with the unorthodox method of being simultaneously at both ends of the stick, he had guessed right. I took it as an expression of extreme trust! That left me with a sense of empowerment beyond the imagined. It also meant that I had already been approved as an able teacher. But how was he capable of evaluating me without having been around for two straight years? That left the Professor with whom I shared intimacy in Monterey... After all, he was the one who recommended me for the position in Rio. I also wondered if the other six teachers had been selected in the same fashion. I would have to wait for answers; obviously, there were still a few items I was required to grasp before "graduation." The most alluring aspect of my "training" was the fact no-one seemed to care about my presence, or what I did with my time. I made no friends, though I didn't wish to push anyone away either. It was a flow that had found its natural course, a latent understanding that we all had a place where we belonged—mine was within the gestative ambiance of the classroom. The extracted knowledge from my solo experiment came as the result of the synthesis of the previous facets of the Program. In some respect, it was a program in more ways than one. I was surprised it took me so long to finally figure it out. The Governor did not have to be present—*he* was the Program! My commitment to pursuing the training to whatever end, had engaged the process that brought me there, in the room where the interactive elements had coalesced into a working whole. The next phase was to convince myself that I had operated simultaneously from the classroom podium, as well as from within the Program. Most likely, I had never been alone! With that stunning revelation reaching all corners of my being, it was no surprise to hear, the next day, that I had been summoned to the dean's office across campus. The tall gentleman once again led me to the concealed office, put a chair in front of the desk, and invited me to make myself comfortable. Gone was the apprehension of the first meeting—I had come full circle.

The Governor went straight to the point. Save for the occasional mishap well within the realm of the expected, I had aced the course, course which, in fact, was the test. There would be no unnecessary graduation, for he and I flew under the radar, as he explained. He further informed me that the Professor and I would meet in Bordeaux where the ship for Brazil was moored, a voyage that would take a lazy month, for, as it turned out, it was a pleasure cruise—arrangements courtesy the Program. I called my parents before boarding; everyone was healthy and all wished me well. I also asked about John; that was when I heard he had been studying in Straßburg the year before, and was presently in Monterey. The Professor made no mention of him—it was just as well.

———— o ————

5 – JOHN

As I previously mentioned, John and I reconnected around twenty years ago in Bayville. When I asked him what he did then, I was immediately alerted to the reality he had no want to divulge that he had been in the Program. I understood that some discretion about what we did was required, but it went further than that; John had cut himself off from the world in a mess of emotional isolation and privation. Only recently did he let me in on the secret, which coincided with his breakup a few months ago. To this day, I still do not comprehend his desire to keep to himself, especially when he should have been aware of my chosen path. I have always been an open book, so a man of his abilities must have known right away what I did. Oddly, I don't think that in spite of having opened the gates, he quite gets at what level in the Program I actually operate. But I could be wrong.

After our reacquaintance, we only saw each other sporadically, until, as I said, he broke up with his life's partner. In general, we crossed each other at art gatherings, concerts, lectures, or wherever events that came to town happened. By then, I had bought a large house in Bayville that I now share with my aging parents. I only met his wife once, but it was on a day I would never forget. For the first time since my work with "identity emissions," I came to an auratic wall. The wife, as I shall call her, was clad in the most impenetrable of layers. Even a well protected soul radiates beyond the shields, but in her case, the wife was akin to an abstraction of energy. She required I put on shields of my own; something I never have a need for. A cold wind blew all the way to my core. She had tried to probe me, but luckily, was only able to reach the lining of a protective overlay that she most likely mistook for my aura. It was a close call, for had I failed, she would have entered the Program from my end. Of course, at that point, I contemplated the ominous scenario that she could have done so using her husband.

So, today, pretending that I feel a sense of responsibility towards John just from the fact we grew up together, would be futile. The past keeps on living its own multiple variations as we speak, and I would be out of my mind to venture into spreading myself thin. John is a case study in need of rescue, but I am under no obligation to distract myself away from the task at hand. For the sake of all things having a place, it suffices to say that he is a convenient, if accidental prop in the story. On the surface we are friends, we eat fish together, and he drives me in his fast, perpetual-motion machine. We share like people do over mundane articles, save for the fact we are both "tale-makers." But even that feels like a commodity in a conversation for the sake of conversing.

Again, how John ended up in the Program is beyond my comprehension. He tries to persuade me that it was a sure-thing with his current "writer," yet it is evident he has managed to alienate him to the point of his wishing to go solo. One can't just blame the "character" for that; the book will go on whether John is in or not. Let's hope that in the worst case scenario, the author has enough of what it takes to pull it off. No, the "swap" is John's fault; he's aware of it as much as we, the Governor and I are. A devil of sort is gnawing at his commonsense, and I wouldn't be surprised if the

Program were to contemplate pulling the plug. Thinking of it, I might even have to do it myself. But until then, I have a responsibility as a kindred "tale-maker," to cast a line in hopes John will catch it. It is protocol in a very loose sense, since generally speaking, a swap of that magnitude, if it were to happen, is hopeless.

So why, you may say, do I even bother having those dinners? Well, it is a question I would ask myself if the Governor and I didn't have an invested interest in the particulars of an improbable scenario involving a renegade agent in the Program. John's behaviour is not common among active members; thus, the possibility of corruption has been anticipated. It's just that corruption often involves a villain—it is when my skills come in, as senior expert in extractive communication.

— o —

I realize that since I started recalling my history with the Program, a cold mist has fallen on my words. The "character's weather" is presently on the side of melancholia from intimate loss that I am not at liberty to discuss, but which nonetheless affects my delivery at the receiving end. I am not naturally a serious soul in spite of my position. I shall forever remain an artiste, with sprite in my stride and boundless playfulness in my interaction with all things. With respect to the "character," who I happen to love dearly, I cannot on my life take away from him the unique emotional signature that makes our communication so precious. We are a team above all, meaning our hearts are in it together. I hope I am making myself clear. This is why John's situation is having an impact—love is no longer there, or worse, was seldom there in the first place. That leaves me with a perplexing question: why? Well, it is better answered by speculating that someone, or something, is invested in a form of sabotage. A process of elimination from the bottom up is what the Governor suggests, and since we always agree with each other, it is the path taken. Obviously, an agent is now acting from within, and of course, it would explain why John was discarded a few months ago—the wife is now inside, doing whatever work she is set on accomplishing. But "inside" may not be totally accurate.

— o —

All of this feels jumbled. John started his morose stage pretty much as soon as he returned to Junction Station, between Emory and Straßburg. By then, the wife must already have been in the picture. It is assuming, of course, that she is the villain or one of his/her pawns. But, since we are to ascertain innocence by subtraction, we have to consider the wife guilty. It led the Governor and I to several forks in the road, each with questions; the first one of which is how, since she wasn't selected for the course, did she manage to know that John was in. The Program was to only be presented as an extra class in diplomacy, as in my case, or creative writing, as in John's. In other words, someone couldn't show interest in it before being chosen and expressly invited. Who told the wife then? Certainly, John could not have been that easily probed; it would have amounted to an item sufficient in making the Program off-limit to him. I guess I am also going to have to look into the selection procedure from that time, and what in the Program potentially allowed for a misread. All could easily become quite complicated, since the admission process was contingent on input from the larger faculty; so, in a way, the Governor could have been handed a bad apple in a moment of distraction, which he is not ruling out. The Program was new at the time, at least in its academic form. The available tracking software was also in its early stages and vulnerable to outside manipulation, but again, it focuses on an outsider... Too many convolutions, it has to be a lot simpler!

— o —

I need to relax the mind. Too much thinking brings me to the brink of confusion and emotional unrest. A good cry is in order. Actually, I have been crying almost daily. It's a rare luxury in a world of many pressures and capricious impulses. I love what crying does to me, the peace it spreads upon its release—the feeling of bruised groundedness. I was speaking of the "character" and of *his* sense of loss—I live in that perpetual state, as my gained knowledge opens greater voids. But it isn't quite the same—still, I relate.

I need the comfort of my house when I feel fragile. My office in downtown Bayville doesn't provide the necessary cocooning; mostly since it is a cover for the Program. With the way I am feeling, anything that strays from simplicity becomes a lie. But around the warmth of the things that I recognize as extensions of myself, and the presence of my parents, the world is complete. It also gets better when the Professor comes to join—which brings me to realizing I have made little mention of him. Yes, he is around, though not often enough. But the little I see of him qualifies as the utmost in joy, as if he made himself bigger by his absence. I am best when I feel like a child.

37

———— o ————

6 – THE CRUISE

The Professor and I waved to the crowd on the dock. We had no friends there, but we waved all the same. Nobody would have known anyway. Bordeaux and my time in France soon faded in the distance.

The ship was immense, a long floating city clad in polished stainless steel and copper. Two of the three spectral chimneys erupted with thick, white clouds, while the other only emitted the undulating dance sent forth by the catalytic burners. She was a grande dame of the seas.

Our room was mid-ship, on the upper story below the lower deck. I didn't fail to notice that someone paid particular attention to making sure we would be comfortable, someone who knew the Professor and I had a history of shared intimacy. It lifted my spirit to be rewarded in such a way. Of course, I shan't go on and on about my relationship with the Professor, how we preferred our sex served, what emotions we held for each other, or whatever inconsequential details about our bodies that might rouse the reader. We were young and passionate—that should suffice! I am far from puritanical, but the sexual descriptive becomes unnecessary fluff in the wrong settings. We see that a lot in "swaps," when the last recourse for a sale is left to the poorly-guised pornographic shock treatment. Enough said!

I could also go in great details about the ship, for there were many mysterious corners within its makeup. No such structure comes without hidden recesses, concealed corridors, rooms away from public sight, and an underbelly teeming with common labourers, operators, and the plethora of bodies without which, should they all suddenly disappear, the ship would stall mid-sea, rust through its hull, and miserably sink. But I shall keep the thought aside.

No, it was the lives of the thousands of voyagers that intrigued me, from the hive-leaning cluster to the individual radiance. I very much doubted the Program did not count on a smidgen of education along the way. This was yet another class, just one not exclusive of an element of extreme, sating pleasure.

The voyagers in question were split between the wealthy idlers, the road-fatigued warriors, the party animals, the giftees, and those who simply wished to reach destination while enjoying a bit of the life. We technically belonged to the latter, though I believed we were two of a kind. After all, the Program wasn't exactly rife with scholars crossing the seas. But short of the playful stretch of the mind—we were in it on par with the rest—a normal couple with over two hundred thousand tons of metal between them and the unforgiving Poseidonian depths.

The cluster element was afflicted with a single, common vulnerability; we were all prisoners of the ship. That was the glue that allowed us to remain civil with each other in a way that wasn't always applicable on solid ground. It did not prevent cliques from forming; after all, the rich had a leaning towards mental inbreeding via a social makeup of verbal and gestural codes, in the form of name dropping, harlequinesque mannerism, and the rarely alluring dribble of obscure factoids about self-serving accomplishments. Strangely, and because of the limited environment, we observed steady defections from those ranks to the more casual spaces of the "commons." It only took a week for the barriers between the various social groups to self-erase. That, we considered, was an important article of hive reflexivity. Roles were no longer dictated by social status, but by specific, shared abilities, and common interests—something that played a lot better in fiction than in real life. In our field, it turned out to be an object of significance, especially from the "tale-maker's" standpoint. If hive behaviour was naturally drawn to harmony while sharing a common vulnerability, and fantasy—in the greater world—was magnetized by similar equity, it meant that the draw was part of the natural order. OK, that was perhaps a bit optimistic, but nonetheless, the concept ended up being an open and enduring item of future teaching.

Against the background of social behaviour, we had the jutting individual, or hero. It was interesting to observe that instead of a desire, or compulsion to lead with what passed, in the eyes of the group, for superior moral fiber, the individual was pulled towards serving the greater good, by sharing what they felt was essential to the betterment of the collective. In choosing so, their fortitude was rewarded with the love of respect.

Naturally, there were a few rotten apples that tried to aimlessly demonstrate that egoism and bad manners could rule. Chance and I heeded not to those factions. Their misplaced sense of power only fed on the fast food of attention, without which they quickly vanished.

There were also the myriad shades in between collective spirit and individual mettle, qualities dependent on time and ambiance to assume their chameleonic stances. In the end, and with nary a policing intervention, we managed to accomplish, in a month's time, what a society without a common dominant threat would in the span of a century, or even, a millennium: the act of deconstructing corrupt social patterns and rebooting the original model. Of course, we were young and eager to set a new, exciting path; soon the card castle would be toppled by the rigid winds of land reality—the life on the ship already drifting towards a forgotten past.

One understands that the Professor and I were also in it for the pleasure. Accordingly, ample humour coloured our observations and theories. Our playful speculations were often inaccurate, or downright silly, but we weren't in it for the sake of a precise science. Let me just say, though, that our inspired, if incomplete, conclusions would soon become fodder to important research.

——— o ———

7 – RIO

The ship berthed in Rio exactly a month after having departed from Bordeaux. I felt a sense of gyration the second my feet touched the ground—the rapid dance of water was called upon by the stillness of solid ground, reaffirming that memory was triggered by absence. But then, an inner voice reminded me that the Earth rotated and orbited at great speeds. It's all relative.

The Chapter building, a converted warehouse whose main access was through an unpaved side alley, stood in the vacuous zone sandwiched between downtown and the industrial district. There was nothing remotely exciting about the neighbourhood, but the energy wasn't as bad as it could have been. The profile of the low surrounding cinderblock structures offered a sense of openness that wasn't totally depressing when the smog was blown the other way. The center was designed to provide lodgings and shared bathrooms for two dozen students on its upper floors, while a series of classrooms, a cafeteria, a large laundry area, small washrooms, as well as outdoor handball and tennis courts occupied the rest. There was also a rammed earth car park in the back. The whole was protected by chain-link security fencing, and monitored electronically. I wasn't sure if the extra protection was the idea of the Program, or if it came with the lease; needless to say, it worried me somewhat. This was so extremely different from Straßburg and Monterey!

The fact was that Rio was one of the few unsafe cities left. Its social makeup was far from exemplary, with its slums attesting to extreme poverty. Ultra-violence borne of desperation and moral starvation, prevailed in the areas beyond the cloistered and heavily patrolled world of the wealthy. I pondered on the reasons for the Program to have chosen that location. Surely, there were other cities with better welcoming arms. But we accepted there was a means to every end, justified or not; so Rio it was!

Our job consisted of going over scheduling ahead of the arrival of the students. We placed ads in the employment section of the local papers, looking at filling the positions of cooks, janitor/maintenance personnel, and the one of much required security. Again, the need for extra vigilance made me queasy, but I trusted the feeling would soon wear off.

We also went over the various curricula applicable to the incoming students. Their individual characters, achievements, and goals were vital to the creation of teaching principles flexible enough to reach each of them equally. Not a simple task, but the first stages of the Program had already oriented them towards a common center.

The Rio Chapter was aimed at catering to South Amerikan students, but it had another goal in mind—that of realigning the social dynamics of the region. It was one of the topics the Professor was to brief me on, before being put in charge of the school. That came as a bit of a surprise, since nowhere in my training had I been made aware the Program concerned itself with regional issues. It seemed to me that it generally chose to isolate itself from its environment. I also wondered why he, the Professor, waited until the last minute to inform me.

Twenty students were scheduled to arrive by all means of transport during the course of the upcoming week. Not all of them originated from South Continent;

three were from the multicultural states of Middle Amerika, the central country between East A., and West A. where I was from, and not to be confused with the Central Union, in between North and South Continents. Two of the three originated from the French States, while the other traveled from the Swedish-speaking Lake Region, above the Germanian Territories. The reason they did not join the Monterey Chapter stemmed from M.A. being, at the time, in a diplomatic freeze with its East and West neighbours—two sister nations.

That is all for the geography!

— o —

Now, how did the Program propose to execute changes in regional dynamics, and how was I going to be the one in charge of making such changes happen without training, or my students knowing about the agenda? Because, that was surely what the Professor implied! He, himself, had no notion of the specific methodology used in influencing a host country's social makeup, all without anyone noticing... Honestly, I thought it was a prank.

I also realized it wasn't.

It was obvious that poverty and violence were the items in need of curbing, which meant the wealthy had to give some back. But to expect an act of generosity on their parts was a bit far-fetched. Yet, deep inside, I sensed there was a way out of the dilemma. Maybe it was the Program talking, for I certainly wouldn't have imagined where to start. The one thing I understood though was that for such a concept to ferment, students and teacher would have to work as a tight group. In that regard, I deemed they deserved to know from the start, period!

My sharing with the Professor, as we lay in bed, was received with approval. He intoned I would have no difficulty figuring it out. I pondered on that while he rubbed my bare back. It felt just right to ease my thinking into bodily pleasure. After all, I had to convince myself that what the Program expected of me was in line with how I actually wanted it done. I was not the kind to sprout a passion out of thin air; it had to gently be extracted out of me, a rub at a time. The Professor knew that—his job was to teach extemporaneously when needed. It made sense in the end—I just had to come up with a way. The one trick was to operate in stealth mode.

— o —

The students were a fun group of equal-numbered males and females; a balance of energies that pleased me greatly. It would make matters a lot easier when the time came to experiment. The Professor left for Monterey the day after the last student arrived. I was officially on my own, with twenty souls looking up to me, little me, barely a couple of years older than them. To say that I wasn't scared out of my mind would have been a bald-faced lie, but I managed to keep my auratic field supple enough to fake a front of integrity. They, the students, probably already saw that I was new at it, but it was to my advantage that they were just as impressionable as I was. I gained countenance merely an hour into my first class. They made it easy on me, like we, a few years back, made it easy on the Professor, who at the time was on his first job at Monterey. What goes around comes around.

It was a good thing figuring out early enough that rigid methodology in Program teaching had nowhere to go. I was a natural improviser, out of which came innumerable ideas, intellectual dares from students, and a sense that we never would come to a screeching halt. I only had to make sure that we didn't stray too far from contributing to the Program's growth. Fluent Portuguese was the one thing required of the Rio students, so as an experiment, we invited—schedule permitting—some of the working crew to the class. We would ask questions/they would ask questions, let's say, all in the form of open-ended interaction—no specific subject. It was play. Metaphorically speaking, the Program stayed in the background, observing. The locals loved it; it gave them a sense of being integral to the family. Perhaps they would tell their children, or other members back home. I stressed on the students to not cross the fine line that would give away the nature of the study. It was an experiment in social behaviour, intrinsic to the Program. Inclusion at the heart level was all that I required.

— o —

I steadily found my footing with both students and workers. The two were, in some way, the unknowing agents of what the Program had required of me. Whether it was a test of endurance expressly prepared for me or not, it didn't matter. I had taken heart to it. Potential was pooling around me, while the students had found their strut in working with the hand. From my perspective, it became clear that what was being carried beyond the Chapter's chain-linked fence, triggered new questions whose answers were awaited by eager ears. Curiosity was the medium that funneled the winds of change. We didn't seek to educate the crew; they sought knowledge on their terms, for reasons that specifically belonged to them. It was the perfect fodder for my classes, while it served my aims very nicely. The process amazed me. I was also conscious that I was becoming one with the Program, not absorbed by it, but given a dimensional frame of reference that I recognized as my own. That was also when I came to understand the Governor's relationship with it. In essence, he was who I would become in time. The thought was both scary and immensely attractive.

— o —

The first wave of change came inconspicuously in the form of a newspaper article, just before the New Year. It wasn't much, just a trickle from the top down. A wealthy family had organized a series of masses followed by buffets for the needy in several parts of town. It wasn't unusual in of itself, for I barely heeded the news when my eyes glanced by it, but a name popped out that changed everything: one of our line cooks also worked for that family.

Naturally, I refrained from taking credit; it would have been way too presumptuous and un-Program-like. But it was a link nonetheless, and a matter of finding its denominator.

As a recap to our relationship with the crew, a couple of items need to be highlighted: we paid them North Continent wages with full benefits, and a mini bus picked them up to and from work, as part of the package. In other words, they had moved a few notches in social ranking, effectively joining the atrophied middle class. Yes, it was a fragile start; anything could have turned on a dime, but just like building a house which first required fence posts and string, or, for the sacred feminine, the vulnerable entry of a newborn into the world, beginnings quickly garnered strength in auspicious settings.

But it was still too early to jump to conclusion. My project needed more glue and pieces to coalesce into a coherent collage. By then, the "merging" had morphed into a semiweekly ritual. The entire crew was present, including the security guard and the driver. It was possible that some of them found our little gatherings odd in a cutesy way, but they came nonetheless. And since it was not a requirement, soon those meetings became their own, as they swiftly overtook the students as mediators. It all worked according to my plan.

It is said that humour is contagious, and so is happiness, or any sustained emotion for that matter. Our crew took their new confidence with them into their world, sending ripples that, in turn, loosened the anchors of the precariously established. Not much, just a bit, but enough for eyes to open, and thoughts to awaken to a figment of new awareness.

I was concerned that if things took off too rapidly, it would jolt the political makeup into reacting. I wanted politics out of the picture. It was a social item of reunification, not one of division. All parties had to be willing—coercion was out of the picture. If the rich were to give back, it had to be the rich wanting to give back. If one did, others would follow as to not be cast apart. Money loved publicity, and if in the process the exploiter looked like a Good Samaritan, all the better. Everybody wanted to be loved, even crooks.

Happen, it did! Without a single battle, various factions of the social realm found their common voice. It would take years beyond that humble beginning to see the completed edifice, but I knew that my students and I had succeeded when the first of the crew gave her notice: she had found a better-paying job, closer to home!

— o —

But with success, even one borne of the shadows, exposure and scrutiny soon followed. After two years in Rio, I received a visit from the Governor. On my recommendation, some of my students went on to be selected to teaching posts in new Chapters. My methods made it to the "manual," while the triumph of my personal assignment carried me to the rarified atmosphere of those who had significantly contributed to the expansion of the Program. But as I said, scrutiny soon came to the security fence of the Chapter building. By then, we had let go of the crew and locked the doors. It was arranged to be that way—Rio had never been more than an experiment.

—— o ——

8 – THE WIFE

Last we met, John and I, his "character" still wasn't accepting his input. I felt inclined to drill him about the wife, but I know too well he would have clammed up. I must rearrange the formula so that he can talk about her without me asking. He confessed that his problems began when she wanted out, while he keeps on insisting depression has nothing to do with it, which is a good thing if we want to go beyond self-pity. But he essentially goes on repeating himself without as much as giving me a modicum of what I want. I like John, but my patience is running out—I need to hear about the wife— that is the primary reason why I am still seeing him over fish. One may say that the way I treat a friend has nothing to do with friendship, but until he allows me in, the undoing is his to bear.

No-one has ever been taken off the Program. It's not something the Governor and I are looking forward to. We don't even know what it will do to John if we take action. Likely, he'll lose his mind, finding himself in a cyclic state of amnesic madness. You can't take away a man's memories without ruining him. I have been schooled and self-trained to recognize John has been the vessel for some yet-to-be-defined ills, with or without his knowing. We are fairly sure those aims are intended to undo the Program, starting with impairing John's abilities to communicate with his "characters," or worse yet, corrupting his entries to catastrophic ends across the line. It is not much for me to go by, but the Governor and I well know there is trouble ahead.

For the time being, John's silence is oddly protecting him from his doom, but it is also bringing that doom closer to him. So, if he doesn't share before we find another means to get to the wife, he is technically finished. One of the few ways out of his predicament would be to collaborate. For that, I would have to reveal my deeper ties to the Program, which is of course out of question for the obvious reason that he cannot be trusted. In other words, to save John, I must break him.

— o —

All John knows about my connection with the Program, besides the both of us having been selected for it a year apart from each other, is that I am one of the early professors, referred to as "Seven." It was knowledge available to all students, so nothing I could do about it. The fact we are both "tale-makers," is the kind of descriptor that adds safe normalcy to our rapport. At John's level, the Governor is a metaphorical authority by which his work is being referenced, an agency of sort issuing licenses on a biyearly basis. John, just as many selected others, is peripheral to the Program; thus, only integral as a permutable cog within its workings. "Tale-making" is a job accountable to performance. In his case, the Program is the employer. How do I know he is not informed of the deeper mechanics he has been serving, as well as benefiting from since college days? Well, nobody is ever entirely sure in the face of the unpredictable, but without factoring that detail in, his behaviour betrays where he's at. His contribution to the Program is well documented—it's barely on the positive side of averaged numbers. Presently, he is floating below the line. He isn't the first one to fall in numbers, but generally, with a bit of readily available retraining, it is an easy fix. John is in the precarious position of not befitting an easy diagnosis, notably, because of his silence about the wife. He is, without a doubt, protecting her, despite the insult he suffered at her hand. It is my responsibility to determine whether fear or the hope of reunification is at the base of his stubborn emotional isolation.

When I looked at him in the eyes, asking if he was seeing someone, he said no. Something is stopping him from dating again. The predictable answer points in the direction of him not willing to let go of the wife. He's still in love, begging for more punishment. It's easy to conclude he is under the spell of delusion, self-made or induced. My take is that he was dragged to the floor on his first dance with her. She was well aware then that he was the perfect tool for the job of getting inside the Program.

Had John been stronger, he wouldn't have found himself here, depending on my energy for support. In some critical regard, it is becoming evident that it was the wife that gave him strength during his training and his successful phase in "tale-making." He collapsed the minute she no longer had a use for him.

— o —

One may ask who the wife is, and how I get to define her emergence and subsequent actions. It's all theoretical for now, but unless the Governor knows something I don't, I am left to assume she is not from our world. Based on John's behaviour, it appears that her arrival is synchronous to the introduction of the Program in Straßburg. For that, she had to be acquainted with the Governor and his work, as well as his decision to bring that ancient knowledge to reality. A few insiders are aware the Governor isn't from here either; thus, it is easily assessed that he and the wife could have crossed paths in other spheres, the mysterious orbs that were the subject of much guilty excitement in the halls of Straßburg. The Governor is asking for a team that will look up our "tale-makers" for information. Presently, John's latest story is being innocently scrutinized by me as we speak. You see, I took the rejection by his "character" as a natural reaction to unsafe contents, indicating that, somewhere in the data, a corruption could potentially be found, and perhaps, with it, the unique signature of the wife. To John's benefit, he is willing to share with me the lead of his aborted tale.

— o —

Through earned intimacy with my "character," I have access to select samples of what he sees. As a matter of fact, I have his permission to tap his experience, and follow some of his reality in real time—something John wouldn't comprehend. It is not my custom to give away names, so there won't be an exception here, but it is to say that, through that channel, I have been able to locate John's "character." I am unable to establish the reasons behind the loss of trust, but location is key. It is now a matter of defining whether John is purposely trying to alienate the author in order to protect his world, consequently sabotaging the wife's work, or going through the motions of doing what is asked of him. The first option is far-fetched, since it would mean he knows more than I think he does. For just a second, I contemplate the possibility of being played—of John and the wife having set me up. As discomforting as the thought may be, I am in no position to leave any stone unturned.

— o —

The breakup point in John's story revolves around a chapter that goes to great lengths at describing a corrupt social media company invested in monopolizing the way people communicate with each other, while injecting profuse amounts of misinformation in order to shape the political landscape for the sole purpose of gaining riches and absolute control. A story of dystopian promise that possibly sounded too unsavoury for the "character" to develop. But John kept on pressing against resistance, which is exactly the opposite of Program protocol. Only madness or desperation could coerce a "tale-maker" into following that path.

If I can't remind John of his obligations to the Program, I can always compliment him on his story-shaping talents, while agreeing his "character" is on an ego meltdown. Since I must get to the specifics of what turned off that author, I have no shame using flattery. If the truth must come out the back door, so be it!

John is halfway through his cod, when I realize the hero of the story has a hidden agenda. Using clever syntactical manipulation, John has spun a subliminal language aimed at turning meanings into their opposites. In other words, bad is good, and the company in question is for the benefit of all, even if the tale says otherwise. From the way I see it, John made the mistake of assuming his "character" blindly trusted his muse. Remarkably, the man is in the habit of cross-referencing intuitive input against a background of experienced truths and deceptions. I wish him well with his version of the story, for I sense John has lost him for good.

Caution dictates that it isn't the time to bring John around to face his inconsistencies. Likely, he is corrupt and should never come near another author again. I will make sure of that! The only thing I presently need from him, concerns the wife. It's no longer too early to put a card on the table—I hit him squarely. I ask him if she, the wife, was ever interested in helping with his work, or if at any time, she had been the inspiration for it. He pauses, looking around the room as if to locate the closest exit, but he instead turns to me with a nod. "Yes, on both counts, though without much success." That's not what I want to hear. The second card is about the true reasons for the breakup—I insist he must trust me if I am to help with his "character."

He finally opens up.

He admits she took him on a never-ending emotional rollercoaster for most of their relationship. When he despaired, she brought him up with charm and promise. Up, she could not stand to see him that way past her own quenched thirst. In the end, which as it turns out was fairly close to the beginning of their relationship, he had become addicted to the pattern. What he mistook for love was his lust for a dominatrix.

I remind him that he is responsible for the outcome of his choices; that surely, there must have been something that she brought to the mix from which he benefited. He keeps on saying that he loved her, that she was extraordinarily beautiful—the best lover he ever had. He should know that I go quite a bit deeper than the skin when it comes to talking about serious subjects, of which I consider a broken heart worthy of my attention. First of all, he married the girl when he was barely out of his teens, so what does he know of sexual encounters and their diversity? And second, "Sorry, beauty is in the eye of the beholder; and 'extraordinary beauty,' on the level of John's experience, sounds hollow!" OK, I got that out of my system—maybe a leftover grudge stemming from having been once in love with him when we were teens. Still, I want to know about the breakup.

So, he goes about telling me that she wanted out because his passions came short of satisfying her, that she was seeing others, men and women, and needed to move in an entirely different direction. But it sounds weak to me, like a step shy of the truth. If John weren't sitting right in front of me, I would swear it wasn't him talking. I just will have to think about it for now.

We almost skip dessert, but I crave something chocolaty. He orders the crème brulée. He finally says that he doesn't know what took him. At last, an item I can relate to!

———— o ————

9 – ADELAIDE

After Rio, the Governor and I traveled together to the Osaka and Moscow Chapters. He wanted to introduce me to the two professors from the original group that I hadn't met yet: "Four" and "Five."

At number seven, I was the last of the first-generation teachers; the Professor was "Six." All of us eventually ended up meeting in Straßburg for a weeklong review of the Program and its future. We unanimously agreed that growth had been astonishing. Already, the next generation of tutors was on its way to open new Chapters, while the bulk of the students continued with the Program in various fields of specialization, of which "tale-making" was testing its first steps.

Since I was out of a Chapter to teach at, the faculty put me in charge of finding a new location to replace Rio. It also had been decided that only two professors were needed in Straßburg. "Three" was available and anxious to work with me, so we rotated the globe and decided on Terra Australis' Adelaide.

— o —

It was always suspect how Chapter buildings materialized, as if they had been placed rather than picked. Adelaide was no different. A space was available on Grand–Boulevard in Seaford, south of town, a kilometre from the beaches, ready for us when we were. I could barely contain my excitement—it was the perfect environment for the Program to thrive; notwithstanding there was no surprise experiment in sight. Safety didn't pose an issue either. "Three" and I self-congratulated on the soundness of our choice.

— o —

The Program didn't snub South Continent. Buenos Aires, in the Argentines, was chosen as a more fitting place than Rio to run a Chapter. Interestingly enough, it was there that John took his first class in "tale-making" under "Eight."

Setting up the Program with "Three" was a breeze. She was so efficient and knowledgeable that she made work look like play. Mind you, the formula wasn't too different from Rio, at the exception that the crew was provided by a separate agency. We told them what we needed and they supplied the personnel. There was no extracurricular activity between them and the student body. A few officials came to verify permits, licenses, as well as inspect living quarters, bathrooms, and kitchens for health regulation conformance. An entity representing the Program was available during the process, her code name: "the Administrator." The Administrator was a local attorney with just the proper leverage to expedite the paperwork. There were no such channels in Rio, in fact, at the time, I wondered if the experiment did not extend beyond the visible. As we know, it did—it was my test.

Before the arrival of the students, "Three" and I made sure to enjoy the beaches and familiarize ourselves with the city where most of the population of South Terra Australis resided. Adelaide charmed our souls to the point of both of us wanting to live there forever. It was the perfect place, never too warm or cold, and the climate was seen as much in its people as out—no promise, no deceit.

— o —

But something odd happened in Adelaide. Just as a reminder there are two sides to every coin, at the start of the second semester, the authorities opened a dubious, not to call it bogus, investigation into the Chapter and issued subpoenas to the faculty. It was clear the intentions were to access our records and scrutinize the nature of our doings. Almost as if he had prepared for it, the Governor was on the scene to pacify hot heads.

Apparently, and I knew how untrue that was, one of our students had written a complaint about a string of psychological abuse at the hand of "Three," followed by allegations of financial wrongdoing, namely, a misappropriation of student allowances.

For one thing there was no such item as a Student Allowance, since tuitions were free and the Program paid for the rest. It was a setup meant to benefit someone bent on seeing the Program jeopardized, at least, as far as the Adelaide Chapter was concerned.

With the help of the Administrator, fevers dissipated rapidly. The authorities issued a formal apology and everything returned to normal. I was left to ponder on what had happened under my watch. Yes, and sadly, there were those who did not want us to exist just because anything that challenged their routine was suspicious. Yet, the investigators would have liked us to believe it was an internal error, but "Three" and I didn't specialize in deep communication to ignore the message in the posturing. Someone in a high place had made an unsuccessful attempt at compromising our work. It was a test, nothing more; a way to gauge the depths of power and influence. There was to be more of it to come.

— o —

Before the incident was relinquished to a dormant place in time, I ran the whole thing in my head. Our group of students, as in most cases, was witty, collaborative, and above all, dedicated to the Program. But I have to admit to a peculiarity as to one of them. He was guarded, even without his shields, which we all took for shyness. Nonetheless, there was an air of melancholia about his person that I now recognize as the same quality found in John much later. Additionally, the head of investigation, a woman in her early thirties, struck me as an overzealous character whose anger was barely concealed by a cover of measured professionalism. She was the one who pointed to the student's complaint, with the obvious, if silent message: "You're so fucked!" An *intimidatrix* by nature, bent on taking wicked pleasure at seeing one fall—good or bad. Back then, I took it that some people had personal issues, not contemplating the possibility of a working organism embedded in the Terra Australis system. But, I had a good reason—they could not have possibly anticipated the creation of the Adelaide Chapter whose information was proprietary to the Program. Only the local authorities could have had a grudge against us for a variety of reasons, not excluding those which could have been generated by some of our hand's malicious gossip in their communities.

Now that I am recalling these memories from my past, I am coming to an intersection of events with the "now": a moody student (Corbyn) and a female of ill intents (Ms. McKenzie Henderson,) stick out like a recipe that strangely resembles the making of John and the wife. I must keep a tab on this.

— o —

The remaining of my stay in Adelaide was uneventful, except when the Professor came for visits and "Three," he, and I had sex together. That was always a welcome high! I managed to make it to Junction Station once a year to see my parents, but the boat trips, express as they were, took away from the time we could have better spent together. In the end, I longed for a closer place to home. I don't know whether it was meant as a gift or not, but the Governor proposed that I dedicate the following year to Bayland, in order to regroup with my thoughts while watering old roots. "The Program needs you there!" That was how he put it.

——— o ———

10 – "A"

It was like taking a deep breath following exertion. It was also the time during which I first met my "character."

"Tale-making" was barely on the radar then, even though it was at the very heart of the Program. The training to it was a slow progression that required passing through all the checkpoints with a clean bill of health. Simply, the course was being built one brick at a time by the most skilled of us. The process of reaching across the metaphorical line that separated realities involved clear, balanced minds willing to take failure and success with equal appreciation. A deep form of meditation had taken us, in the early days, into the cavernous network of the psyche, where we met our first travelers. Though it was clear that the goal was to eventually connect with the other side (or, other sides,) we only concerned ourselves with getting closer to the threshold. The concept of dictating data to "characters" in the form of stories, or assisting them in writing their own, was not breached yet. As I was saying, we were in the process of building that course, and it took years before I, at last, found the space to connect.

By then, I knew what I was looking for; a sympathetic soul that was just as curious as my own. I was met with failure after failure, to the point, I confess, of doubting my own training, which as I learned later, was part of the list of accepted failures itself. No-one can say the Program is not accommodating! But then, I sensed a pull, or rather, I heard a call. Someone had already reached their personal threshold, not knowing they were there, as I discovered soon enough. We had figuratively been facing each other for a "good while" before I came free of my hypnotic stance of self-criticism. Naturally, we couldn't see through the opacity of the shield, and I am to this point, still unsure how much he was aware of my presence. But that's a detail open to evaluation when the definition of awareness is at best subjective. All that mattered was the call. He was my first "character," and because of it, I shall from now on refer to him as "A."

I knew "A" had sensed that I was around when our blind encounter became, ever so briefly, enrobed in stillness. There was a hint of desperate vulnerability that bled through, informing me he was ready to accept my existence to its fullest—something I was far from expecting. Miraculously, he trusted me instantly, believing he had connected with the sacred feminine within the self. I found the item endearing in a way that shames me today; my arrogance had made me insensitive to the fundamental truth that he held. But it took me the longest to come to terms with the fact someone had met me halfway without the Program. He didn't seek to know who I was; his faith in me was all the anchor he needed. He had called for help, ready to heed the message, leave the past behind, and enter the path to a new personal journey. That was one of the heaviest lessons I had to learn in all my time with the Program. I had pitted hubris against courage. When I realized the Governor had seen the corruption before it manifested, which was cause for him to send me home, my world collapsed. I was back to square one, a younger me roaming the corridors of the Straßburg Chapter, in awed incomprehension before the knowledge that lay ahead. In a fit of self-loathing, I abandoned both the Program and "A."

That also was part of the teaching.

I took to heart that I was free from my immediate past. I did not return calls from the Professor—he had stopped existing in heart and mind. I had turned my memories of Straßburg and all the other Chapters, of my accomplishments and my steady climb within the Program, to a labyrinthine reality best avoided. My nerves came unraveled as I slowly fell into intense melancholia. I refer to it as my personal Dark Ages.

— o —

During that time within which I refused to contemplate depression, I traveled the Pacific Coast from Upper North Continent, to the borders of the Central Union. I passed Monterey twice with nary a thought for the Professor. In the end, all I wanted was to be home with my parents, working the garden with my mother and helping dad with whatever project took his fancy. Ironically, I lived on Program money saved over the years—quite a lot of it—with some of which I bought the house in Bayville. I decided to move into my own place upon realizing that my clutter did no longer belong to my parent's home. I could still spend time with them whenever I or they so desired.

It was likely that loneliness had something to do with me wishing for the company of "A." I probably had shattered his trust, but I was coming in with a clean slate, ready for my slice of humble pie. When I couldn't perceive his presence, I panicked. I wildly imagined that my rejection had caused him critical harm. It was my turn to do the calling. The awakening was brutal. I was in tears, feeling the deeper ramifications of my recklessness

64

to their fullest. I had betrayed the most precious thing in my inner world to now face the mortal silence. Every day, I called to no avail. I surrendered to the notion he was dead. My heart hit bottom; the pain was unbearable. It was no stranger I had killed, but a vital part of the ability to love the self and all things. I felt on the edge of finishing the carnage by contemplating total annihilation. That, I think, was what did it. I heard a voice, or was it a thought, a feeling, whatever... All I knew was "A" was behind that threshold, and all I craved were his trust and love. I begged for forgiveness only to realize he was too hurt to hear my plea. He had crawled one more time to the line in the hopes his faint call for help would be heard. It would have been his last.

I heard the rale of my words as if they had come from a hidden place. "Oh, loved one, I'm here!" the voice said, again and again. I cried the tears of outrage at my own shortcomings. It was the work of irresponsibility that lay between us, the carelessness of those imbued with misplaced powers. When I heard his whispery "Please, stay with me," I shut my thoughts and held an imagined "A" against me. We both fell asleep.

— o —

Now, describing the evolution of my relationship with "A" may be lost in translation. We were not physical beings in the sense that we could touch each other, but we existed in an environmental commonality that allowed us to perceive our interaction as if it had been physical. In other words, powerful-enough through-prints were made across the opacity of the shield, in the form of thoughts, images, bodily sensations that, with time, became as vivid as the real thing. I saw that his world was similar to mine, the same bay with the same towns, but with different names. His air was polluted, but it was worse to the north and south. His land cried, and the animals at the border of his forests were all experiencing despair. More critical, yet, were his people, suffering at the hand of an incontrovertible ruin of their own making. "A" needed to feel that there was a greater reality to his picture of doom, a reassurance that love was still at the base of all things, and that there was still significance to his life. "A" is the quintessential artiste who appreciates life in all of its creative manifestations. He composes music, plays the instruments he makes, a soul that sees his work as a healing force. I have come of assistance to many of his projects. The writing is of course what I am the most invested in—he lets me in, while taking his position as a trustful observer of the process. I adore him.

When we linked for good, the second time around, his torment was such that it was hard to imagine how he made it to the threshold. What saved him from an early demise was his blind reliance on the self. He found strength where others dared not go—in fear—and by answering solely to the man in the mirror, he took accountability for all of his life's shortcomings—no blame, no remorse; qualities I found very attractive.

My influence worked miracles, though I can hardly take credit for it. Through our connection, he harnessed renewed strength and hope, all the while taking me in as a vital part of his larger self. I was the friend, the companion, the private lover to whom he answered with kindness when *she* called, for she did—often.

I cannot stress enough that "A" saved me from my own despair. I mean, I was contemplating suicide for

Christ's sake! For lack of better words, we were both in the process of dying.

Whether the Program deems kinship a necessary item of true connection or not, it's all figurative, but I haven't come across another "tale-maker," throughout the entire Program, whose "character" has had such a cathartic effect on their experience. While alone in my bare house in Bayville, I cried for days on end from joy and sadness alike. I lived the loss of my gains through every shade of regret, shame, injustice, whether imagined or not. My meeting with "A" had taken me to an empty room, deep inside the Program. To this day, no other has ever entered it.

———— o ————

11 – CONVALESCENCE

It took months before I regained my balance. Meanwhile "A" and I had started with short stories to set off the pace. At first, I felt more like an observer than a narrator. It was because I hadn't fully comprehended my role. The source of a story could either be "A's" or mine—his, when based in his personal experience, and mine, as it is presently the case, with something entirely out of his realm. A "tale-maker" can either provide data or guidance. In the end we must work together. The goal, as far as the Program is concerned, is healing. In the ideal scenario when a story becomes the end result of shared work, nirvana can be reached. But I'm ahead of myself!

As I said, it took me forever to regain my wits. I hadn't heard of the Governor or anyone at the Program. The Professor stopped calling, while "Three" forwent the hope of working together again.

I drove around Bayland in the old hydromobile, taking "A" with me, whenever I could, to deserted beaches, hidden trails, and small tucked-away communities in the coastal range. At thirty-thousand, Bayville was the biggest metropolis in the county, so it was easy to find privacy outside its limits. When I say I took "A" with me, I don't mean that he sat in the passenger seat, but I still deemed he was my co-pilot. I was inspired by these short trips, willing to turn them over to him as fodder for his writing. Mostly, he stored the data for later use. Only when I considered my experience pertinent enough to assist in the healing of his world, did I press him on taking it to the page.

As I mentioned earlier, much is lost in translation when it comes to my story with "A." The ethereal quality of our relationship does not easily subject itself to words. For the sake of a necessary comparative, he was me, as I was him—the two sides of a coin. But only at the particular threshold at which we met did that apply, since we couldn't exist in each other's worlds, at least, not then.

— o —

Came the time at which I felt I had been disconnected from the Program, or rather, the feeling was one of ebbing, like a veil being slowly dragged away from under me by invariable inertia. I intuitively knew my choices were the force that could change that perception, but I didn't do anything about it. I waited until I confronted the last of my fears. That came rather fast.

My relation with "A" was intrinsically tied to the Program. With it falling into numbness, so did my sense of connection with my "character"—I would eventually lose him as well. Oddly, the reminder did not come from the Program, but from "A," who, in a surprise-moment of lucidity on my part, came across warning me that I was slacking at my responsibilities. It was oh so clear: "Do your fucking job!" I was jolted out of my stupor like a dislocated puppet whose strings had been pulled from above. I straightened my metaphorical spine into action, finally aware that the sound of the alarm wasn't part of the dream I had mistaken for the waking state. My love affair with "A" had made me blind to what had brought him to me in the first place. Bayville had become a zone of dangerous comfort, where "A" could only exist as a memory that I would keep alive only by losing my mind.

In a flash, I saw myself as an old lady conversing with her taxidermied cat. It scared the living shit out of me—I picked up the phone and rang the Professor.

70

—— o ——

12 – RE-ENTRY & EXIT

Within days of the call, I was back in Monterey, at a café terrace, in the company of the man I had once shared a consummate affair with. He was relaxed, pleased to see me, the way one appreciates a moment in the sun.

He had asked me to come over to share my last year away from the Program and what I had learned from it. I needed to be face to face before getting straight to the point. Was I still in the Program or not?!

He looked at me with distinct amusement, as he brought to my attention minutiae that had escaped me: for one, I never was out of the Program; only my perception of it and "A" had been altered by my inner conflicts. We all had them in direct proportion with the task at hand. He said that much had been expected of me over the years, and thus it was inevitable I would one day come to a place of evaluation of the self. But he made it clear that at no time did anyone ever imagine I would be reaching a milestone. Namely, I was first to breach the theoretical barriers of two worlds and enter in an alliance with an alien entity, but the most peculiar thing: one from an "unfriendly" reality. On top of it, it was inconceivable that I would meet with someone as available as "A." Calls were heard across that line—mostly aimed at various imaginary beings, or icons—but never one directed at a specific consciousness on our side. As I understood it, "A's world" was considered a hard nut to crack, one long watched by the Program, and deemed a terminal reality. My breakthrough was received with open arms, but it came with an element of concern: "A's" world was on the brink of tipping the scales towards a fall into an irremediable darkness. To save it would demand unimaginable talent and resources, while posing danger to the Program via the vulnerability of the threshold. Only an extremely skilled "tale-maker" would attempt making contact. Thanks to "A," I was the oblivious candidate.

I was "diagnosed" with having been exposed to the excessive negativity of "A's world" via my intimate relationship with him, which explained my early rejection of all things Program. I didn't like the sound of it, but I had to abide by the reality of my irrevocable loss of balance. I have to admit that I was a mess back then, a mess caught in the Janette Trudy Smyth dilemma.

— o —

I stayed in Monterey for a few days, enjoying my reacquaintance with the Prof. It was nice to again belong, but I was anxious pick up where I had left off. I had no doubt the Governor had something is store for me; it was just a matter of time before he would show up—not that his absence necessarily meant he didn't keep track, as I discovered in Straßburg while self-training for the professorship. On my trip back home, I pondered on the ways to not let myself be affected by "A's world." I had no intention of letting him go, but I couldn't let the love between us destroy us. I barely finished my thought when I realized what I had done—a part of me had crossed, while I had let an equal part of him in. No-one's fault really; it was the way we survived at that critical moment of dying. It was just a matter of disconnecting the ambience of his world, and disassociating from having confused his emotions with mine. We didn't have to let go of the embrace—we barely needed to shift position.

— o —

While "A's world" was similar to mine in many respects, some details unmasked radical differences in our histories. For example I saw horrific pictures of war—twice in a row—that never punctuated my global reality. Our last major conflict was in 1870. So, I assumed he had to know that as well. Of course, I recognized assumptions mostly came at the price of being wrong. I couldn't see what he saw the way he saw it—I was too familiar with my own reality to see the alienness of it. But whatever it was he witnessed on my side, I hoped he took it back and put it in words. I strived to give him the hope that his world could be healed from its wounds. But the fact remained that the Program wanted to exercise caution.

When I returned from relieving myself at one of nature's pit stops, I found the Governor sitting in the front passenger seat of my auto, his long legs practically folded against his chest.

I cannot say that I didn't expect him, but the settings were particularly odd, as I had just decided on a change of underwear and was carrying the suspect pair, ready for the swap. I had to excuse myself momentarily before he could get my attention—one way to break the ice! Of course, he ignored the whole thing.

The point was that I was needed back in the Program, but I was far from expecting that headquarters awaited me in the least expected of places: Bayville—the Bayville of "A's world."

The Governor did not bother reading my reaction; he had no interest in superficiality. I was back on the job because he had no doubts I was ready. According to him, I had satisfied all the requisites for officially returning to work, and now that I had made solid contact, he wanted me to see "A's world" for what it was.

To my surprise, headquarters was my home, the one across "the bridge." The Governor demanded that I ignore how we got there—I had blacked-out and that was all I needed to know. Looking outside the window of the living room, which now was an office, I was stricken by a sense of utter disorientation. For one, the noise from traffic was insane, and then the smell emanating from the odd, angry autos chasing each other out there, immediately nauseated me, even though everything was closed. I couldn't see myself stepping outside the building—I was terrified. I had never heard of fire engines, ambulances, or police cars, so when they came flying by the house, I thought it was the end of me. The Governor waited patiently for me to settle down.

— o —

It wasn't like Rio wasn't noisy or polluted, but this was happening in Bayville, a stone's throw from by place of birth. Needless to say, I feared to imagine what it was like in "A's" Rio!

My bed and bath were under the gambrel roof on the third floor. The Governor kept his quarters by the office. I slept the sleep of the dead. I woke up, my head in a fog, which thankfully muffled the reality of outside. I couldn't believe my house had morphed into Program headquarters across the thin wool of illusion. A blackout, the Governor had said—induced by whom?! But I knew this was the wrong question to ask him over coffee... I hoped there was coffee in "A's world"!

After a well deserved shower and a change of clothes, (I couldn't bother asking myself how my stuff had followed me across whatever it was,) I met the Governor in the office where a pot of coffee was brewing. From among the first sensory messages allowed to penetrate the clutter of my confused mind, the smell emanating from that pot promised a decent start. The taste, on the other hand, could have improved. But I assumed we were not there to examine the science behind a perfect cup.

The Governor, who wasn't known for answering questions, came straight to the point. Since I had been pioneering "tale-making," my presence here was to strictly explore. He insisted my education had exceeded the capacity of the Program, and that our presence in "A's world" was to purvey to its expansion. Headquarters was a misnomer for "base," for there were only the two of us across the line. The synchronicity of my home serving that function was answered in simple terms: it was meant to be—just like the rest!

The items of exploration were categorized in sections: environmental health, technology, culture, philosophy, the psychology of individual and mass-hypnosis, social structure and its redundancies, species displacement, and tribal reality. Subcategories were in numbing numbers. It somewhat helped that "A's world" was in the image of our own, assuring us we would likely be dealing with comparative differences only.

Talking of "A," I was at no time to connect in person—the implications were too dire to justify the thrill.

In spite of the slight disappointment, I perfectly understood my responsibilities in regard to the dangers that posed. It also meant that I would have to resist powerful impulses in the case of an accidental encounter. As the Governor stated, and based on my allegiance to the Program and its expansion, I was the only one capable of making it happen. In his views, there had never been failure on my part—only the incontrovertible dynamics of success. Both the subliminal warning and the compliment were well received. Following two more days of details briefing over IDs, bank accounts, and whatever a spy's panoply and mission consisted of, I was told I was on my own. The Governor would fetch me in due time.

The announcement hit me like a brick in the face. I wholly awoke from the numbness of my disorientation to experience heightened panic. It was not a dream; I was reduced to a diminutive object placed among infinite unknowns and dangers. I was scared out of my mind!

———— o ————

13 – BAYVILLE 2

Bayville 2, as I shall call it, wasn't just minutely different from my own. Fundamentally, and because of the resemblance, it was made all the more alien to me.

For one thing, I was unfamiliar with pumps at which autos filled their tanks. I walked to one of them, called Renner 91, and it smelled awful of acrid vapours. What was it that they put in their vehicles instead of distilled water? Water was nearly free, but that which they named "fuel," based on my fresh introduction to the dollar, was dear. In my world, the currency unit was the Pacific Pound, or "Pod" for short—so very divergent!

I spent the following days studying "fuel," its history, as well as its social and environmental impact. It was a tragedy on a grand scale—so many innovations lost, and at so much cost in damage and wars, when so much of its insane profits went to so few. Right there glared a basal corruption: greed.

Greed in my Bayville was at the level of benign inequities. An obese child was thought to be greedy; a fisherman exceeding the regulated catch was another. Energy-wise, Bayville 2 reminded me of Rio, where I saw what I considered extreme imbalance, but even there, we were able to make subtle changes with just a few of us at the Program. At that moment I realized how the Governor had set me up. He knew all along that I would need skills when the turn for serious work came around. My mind was caught in a whirl!

I bought the smallest auto I could find, a little Honda that had the decency of not being too greedy on fuel. Still, even shiny new, it smelled of bad combustion. Another word they used for fuel was "gas," which at first didn't make any sense to me. Perhaps they meant it was so volatile a fluid that they might as well call it a gas. So, from then on, every time I would "fuel up," I wore a chemical mask purchased at a general store. By the way other "fuelers" looked at me, I feared that I had been compromised and that one of their scary policemobiles would race to pick me up—but it didn't—I was just crawling out of my skin. I was in a state of shock; a condition I hoped would leave me with time.

In the midst of getting gradually settled into my new assignment, I almost forgot about "A." I wondered if we were still connected, if by some sort of fluke, physical proximity had damaged the link. I let the thought follow its course: it wasn't the right place and time to reminisce about our relationship. I took it as just a variance on the perceptual scope—there was no longer a need to share between worlds since we lived in the same one.

Little Honda and I drove to Junction Station 2, on our first exploration trip outside the city. Unlike my house, my parents' was nowhere in sight. In its place stood an ugly, red plywood low structure with a couple of greedy open-backed lorries parked in front of it, idling in a mess of rattling parts and black exhaust. I waited until I saw four men loading motorized tree cutters in their vehicles, and leaving in a huff of disgraceful remarks about bitches. I was sorry the energy of my parents and their little farm had been unable to bleed through. I cried all the way out of town—"A's world" was awful.

Since logic dictated that I stay away from making acquaintances, my only friend was Little Honda. She and I even drove all the way to Monterey, with a stop in San

Francisco. At least the names were the same, but SF stuck out as being way beyond my tolerance for noise pollution and hyper-activity. It was there that I heard about AIDS, a horrific terminal disease that was ravaging gay [sic] communities. I also sensed, there, that white people were scared of coloured ones to the point of hatred. I had so much to understand about that version of humanity.

In "A's world," I felt like a scared child trying to comprehend injustice, anger, and the plethora of emotions that churned within me. It was my reality gone mad starting a century ago, before fuel, the misuse of colliding atoms to evil ends, and the rampant reliance on logical fallacies as a way of manipulating the crowds in the so-called free world. It was all empty promises, lies, deceitful advert—it was as if my world, instead of healing itself from previous wounds, had made the choice of falling deeper into illness. From that perspective, I thought I had found Hell!

But in spite of it all, Little Honda and I saw what could be saved. The roots of felled ancient trees had sent new shoots skyward, birds sang amid the brush, here and there people still whistled, shared, and loved; flowers, mushrooms, and other plants reclaimed the scarred land, unflustered by the onslaught of destruction. Hope hadn't died yet, and that was a beautiful thing—even more beautiful than the beautiful things in my world. The awakening to the emotion was astonishing—I had found a moment of happiness among the misery, in a heightened form of joy. I parked Little Honda along the Avenue of the Giants, walked into the ancient forest, rested my back against an immense redwood tree, and cried all the tears bottled in my heart since my arrival. When it was over, it started all again—I was salt among the sorrel.

My little mechanical friend and I retuned to town. I parked her in the corner of the garage that I had arranged specially for her. I believed she was happy. I took care of her since my dad has taught me a thing or two about autos. Of course, she was somewhat messier than the hydromobiles of my world, but I loved her all the same. I was recently informed that the rubber of her tyres, the seats, and the console were made of the same stuff fuel came from: crude oil. I was mesmerized at first, but then I learned about all the other things made from it. Crude oil was what we called "earthblood" back home, a product we used to heal skin ailments with. I almost had second thoughts about gas, or gasoline as it turned out, but I remembered the damage. It didn't change how I felt about my mechanical friend though.

— o —

One evening, I did the mistake of contemplating my socializing prospects. I went to a downtown bar and sat at a lone table. I agreed to something recommended by the waitress, a colourful cocktail with a little umbrella sticking out of it—it was darling!

I was in the midst of enjoying being around people while sipping my drink, when a rude gentleman sat in the chair across me to engage in conversation. He was drunk, but in him, instead of celebration, I perceived something dark, as if the alcohol had turned him around into something he normally wasn't. Nobody had ever called me "baby"; it was a terrible way for a man to address a woman. He also ventured to ask me where I was from, as if he meant it, but all I could feel was ill-intent, an irrational lust for my flesh without the customary love.

There was no doubt in my mind he disrespected women, even worse, he despised them. He was afraid of the sacred feminine, and all the more dangerous because of it. I knew that if I got up and left, he would follow me, so I sat there, pretending I was listening to his diatribe. I ordered another cocktail to calm my nerves. He insisted on paying for it, assuring to himself a special pass into my favours. The more I felt oppressed and paralyzed, the tighter the trap closed around me. I excused myself for the bathroom in hopes of breaking the spell, but I was pushed out of my allotted time by the perpetual line forming at the door. The man was waiting, ascertained of his advantage over me, ready to take me wherever people like him lured their preys, wherever he would fuck me without love, and loathe me for my shame. So I did the only thing a desperate woman could think of at the time, I threw the content of my glass at his face and ran out of the bar. He went after me, but was met at the door by a group entering the premises. I lost him at the end of the alley, as I merged with Second Street pedestrians. I went straight "home," making sure I was not followed. As I double-locked the entrance, I wondered how much longer my nerves would be able to sustain the demands of the assignment. Unfortunately, all depended on the Governor's return for my rescue.

— o —

It was at that point that I began longing for "A." All I wanted was the comfort of his presence at our usual meeting place, by the threshold of our worlds. I didn't know how to get there anymore, for the corridors to it were in my reality—I was now in his. We no longer were facing

81

each other, but walking a matched set of parallel tight ropes that could only meet at infinity—in other words, nowhere safe in reasonable time.

— o —

I spent each day studying the items on the list, doing research at the library where I spent most of my afternoons. The year was 1984, my thirtieth. I felt it the strongest of any others, as the effect of my isolation combined to the coming of the fall. On occasion, I took Little Honda to the university to deeper investigate the misaligned mechanics of the world that was in the process of absorbing me. I wanted so much to make friends, touch someone, share my stories from yonder... At times, I found it pathetic that I should be left talking to my mechanical sidekick, my one trusted friend. It was well known that madness often ensued such traumatic contact with alienness. I felt for the poor souls that lived on the streets, engaging with imaginary beings; yet their conversations so real and focused—did they too come from other places?

A lot of what I learned was very depressing. The future of "A's world" resonated of mine's past. Yes, our histories meshed until the cutoff of 1870 when, in my world, the United States, which had joined the French against Prussia, were defeated and had to surrender the central swath of the Union to the victor. The country was further divided into separate nations, East and West Amerikas, as the result of which economic and social structures were realigned. Which also explained why the Standard Oil of Ohio Company never formed, as it did in "A's world" under John D. Rockefeller. In other words, the similarities between our respective realities ended when the choice was made to join France, which was followed by the replacement of the oil industry with less environmentally offensive resources. For us, it was the beginning of sustainability, while oppositely, the attacks on the natural world, here, were exponentially increased to purvey to the unquenchable thirst of those who sought riches and control. It went on and on in all areas of industry, finance, of the military complex and politics: obscene wars, corporate crime, censure of artistic expression and freedoms, massive assaults on traditional medicines, the systematic poisoning of crops and foods with subsidized chemicals whose test results were heavily manipulated, the ravage of virgin forests, et cetera, et cetera! I was nauseated from all the greed and lies, as well as the total apathy of the masses, as if the human race, instead of choosing to evolve, opted for global suicide, taking with it the rest of the planet. How on Earth could little me and "A" hope to fix that kind of a mess—was the Governor out of his mind?!

It was the general feeling at the end of each report.

— o —

But back to "A"! Not hearing from him eroded my confidence in our alliance. Last we disconnected, we both almost died. I was hoping that by me being in his world, he could sense I was there, close by. Of course, at the risk of repeating myself, we couldn't meet in person; plus, I wouldn't have known where to start looking for him, since we obviously didn't share addresses.

The chance for an encounter, as I learned later, was highly improbable. Contrarily to my belief that "A" lived in his version of Bayland, he had only visited the area once. The mistake stemmed from me misreading the energy field, and overlaying my reality onto his. He, at the time, resided in San Francisco.

— o —

Bayville 2 was a logging town, one whose future precariously balanced on the fact trees were a finite resource, which in the face of poor forest management, were to become an even scarcer commodity—another hypocritical aspect of my research. It always ended up with lies passing as truths—grotesque methods that kept on gnawing at my intelligence. These people had lost their commonsense! Anyway, the city was on the brink of financial collapse, but instead of seeing it as an ill, I foresaw hope in the form of a beneficial change—when greed could no longer be fed, greed left town—or died.

I was doing my best to forage for the positive at the bottom of the pile of my daily discoveries. It was not easy considering I had already seen the alternatives. But there were positives, and yes, there still was hope for "A's" old world. Nevertheless, the way I calculated it, if by the year 2025 these positives didn't congeal into a whole, there would be little chance for a reversal. Forty years weren't much, but it was feasible. One challenge was to define the trigger mark for that reversal, which could be anywhere between now and then, as I saw it.

My train of thoughts took me back to my reality circa 1870. No-one before me had ever been in a position to ask the question, "What sparked *our* choice for taking the better path then?" That query rang like an answer in the making—whoever pushed for the US to aid France in its war against Prussia stood at the pivotal point. I was in the wrong place to do the research; yet, being on the wrong side was what brought me to it. Irony never rested.

— o —

I abandoned my hopes of connecting with "A"— time would tell. Instead I secured my allegiance to the mission by finally settling into my role. Little Honda and I did the rounds of hiking trailheads. I studied the trees, listened to birdsongs, smelled the winds for pollutants, gazed at the stars from the top of mountains, met with startled black bears, hissing rattlesnakes, skittish deer, and suspicious lynxes; witnessed salmon run up the creeks and hundreds of majestic moths and butterflies flutter in the light of moon and sun. The more I advanced into the deep, the more my militant self rose. There was no way I was going to let such resilient beauty die—my place was defined—I was resolute to join the resistance. Greed was on my radar.

On the return from one such trip, as I locked the doors and entered the office, the Governor was there, waiting for me. The time had come for me to go home!

It was with tears in my eyes that I said goodbye to Little Honda. I trusted she understood.

——— o ———

14 – THE BRIDGE

I still didn't comprehend the process of crossing over, and the Governor wasn't into telling. Once more, I blacked out and found myself in the living room of my "real" house. I looked out the window; gone were the policemobiles and the sickly roar of motors. I opened the lower sash to breathe the air—it was perfect—every bit as good as the best in the other place. I was relieved but sad. It didn't matter how bad it was at times. It could be said that I lived in a perpetual state of Stockholm syndrome— it was particularly true of the world I had left and whence the term came. I discovered what it was to be a prisoner of misery to the point of missing it when it was gone. In a world weak on fundamental goodness, the act of living came to encompass what was worth to live for—the preciousness of inner love.

The Governor and I went over my reports, but he already knew what they contained without bothering reading them. What was important to him was the fact I didn't require being rescued before I was done. I had completed my assignment when I made the decision to work for "A's world." By then, I had fully come around, my fears replaced by empathy towards what could be saved in the human soul. It was no longer about the outer me, but the inner one that saw the deeper meaning of life in all of its forms. "A's reality" did not need to become ours, it simply deserved to move in the direction of its best foreseeable outcome—that was what the Program was ultimately designed for. I was the trigger capable of initiating change, and "A" was the likely reason for it.

Having understood what I had bargained for, I refocused my attention onto "A." The Governor had left for yet another of his mysterious destinations. It was clear that for the time being, my teaching credentials were not needed. I had graduated to the ranks of "designers," the rare few who saw through the eyes of the program, sharing its peripheral vision and anticipating its pressing needs. There was only one group between us and the Governor—the "Overseers," who made sure all things were as they should be.

— o —

It took me nearly a month before I sensed "A's" presence behind the threshold. It was not as strong as during our periods of intimacy. I understood why he would be reluctant to get close again, for my absence must have felt like abandonment. I was wrong—within days, we had bridged the gap!

From that point on, it became easier to navigate data without being afflicted by cross-shield negativity. My immersion in "A's world" had given me the perspective I needed to remain focused without losing myself in my "character's" emotions. Not all was right with him, but he let me in just enough for me to sense my presence was a soothing force on his psyche. Meanwhile, the writing resumed, starting with letters to friends, family, and lovers. I was strictly an "overseer," advising on the importance of authenticity, on how to recognize hidden agendas and projections—both killer agents of sincerity—but above all, how to not get too attached to intellectual values, or lured by the false assumption that smart words had leverage in conversation. But "A" wasn't easily convinced, so I can't say that I always succeeded. Overall, my advice was well received, allowing the message to go through.

— o —

But there's more to "tale-making" than either coming up with stories or assisting in their building. Specific messages must be encrypted in the syntax to draw the reader's attention. It is not trickery—they are the healing agents, the evolution clauses, the caution markers.

The syntactical arrangement is made of layers, of which three are respectively in charge of visuals, audibles, and cadence. They are intertwined languages perceived at their own unique frequencies, which must resonate in chorus to make a whole; meaning that the eyes, beyond seeing, can also hear, feel, and smell. It is the responsibility of the "tale-maker" to make sure that each of these elements carries its part of the message. In time, as the "character" evolves, he or she may take over that task.

In my experimental role as pioneer in cross-world communication, I am the first ever to tell my real story and to expose the existence of the Program. Others have, at times, hinted at uncovering our work, but mostly in the form of innuendos. The only reason why this is possible is because of "A." Without him, a great void would exist in the place of this monologue. The experiment I speak of is not just an exercise in advanced "tale-making," but part of the continuous coding that allows for the Program to expand—coding, in this case, being the essence of my personal experience. I hope I am making myself clear, for it is important to understand the distinct dissimilarities between conventional binary coding and the more complex and organic stuff of experience, fed to an amenable gestalt of consciousness such as the Program. The entire first part of my teaching was on how to become incrementally integral to it. In that way, I couldn't see the larger picture until I familiarized myself with it naturally. I was made constitutive through my conviction that the student body benefited the Program's greater purpose, a purpose that was to become obvious over the years. I was, from the start, informed of the experimental nature of my schooling and assured that I would remain intrinsically tied to the natural order. I hadn't joined a sect bent on ruling the world, as one of the trial students had alluded to once, but an organization intent on creating harmony across a vast area of consciousness. There were no promises nor were there lies. Only once did I doubt my place—I was young.

— o —

For the time of my early phase at "designing," I remained in Bayville. My stay in "A's world" had inspired me to let go of my downtown office and move its contents to my living room. After all, I had far more space than I needed, and my parents were still in love with their property in Junction Station to contemplate moving in with me. It also brought me closer to the reality across the shield, to the point of expecting finding Little Honda in the garage—I generally cried when that happened. I imagine I was trying to blur the line without knowing, or if I knew, I ignored that I did. As a matter of fact, it was exactly what was expected of me—to create a permanent link between worlds.

89

I had come to understand that a physical bridge between realities was only possible via first exploring the strata of the soul and laying markers. But just like two feuding countries in the process of re-opening their diplomatic channels, it took equal effort on both sides. My role was to instigate such effort on "A's," by making him aware of the importance of his participation in building that bridge. But "A," who was a surprise in many ways, reacted by pointing that he was the one who called first; hence, his side of the span was awaiting my half. It was a humbling realization, as I had so conveniently forgotten that we were the ones who had originally written off his world as terminal. But this time, I wasn't flaking—I hastened with the process of turning my house into a revolving door. Like that, I would be able to cross-reference my work at will. All I had to do was figuring out how the Governor had brought the two of us across.

It was a lot more complex than I first thought.

— o —

The complexity in question was in having to create a bridge from scratch without knowing the first thing about it. The way I saw it, such a bridge could only respond to the unique signature of its maker, which partially explained why it came at the cost of a blackout for users like me. That being said, I had to start somewhere, so I aimlessly rationalized. For example, I contemplated the ideal scenario of two builders standing at each end, like, let's say, "A" owning the house in Bayville 2; it then would have been a given that inner and outer channels should align perfectly, but it obviously wasn't our case. As mentioned earlier, he lived in San

Francisco at the time—something I was in no position of knowing then.

In recap, my building of the bridge was what most likely drove my "character" northbound. But that wouldn't happen until years later—six to be precise. So, fate had it that I should be left to figure it all out on my own, for the only bridge "A" could afford to work on was the one that connected us at the heart level.

I had persuaded myself that both my inner connection with "A" and the Governor's accessways were natural counterparts—I was wrong. One was a bridge between souls, the other, a portal between two physical planes. In reality, I should have heeded the fact that one was already there—the threshold at which my "character" and I met—while the other remained a mystery, merely a concept at its embryonic stage. I had been misled by fleeting, random assumptions around the two houses. As I said, I rationalized, mostly out of a sense of panic.

— o —

I spent long hours in the office trying to figure out a possible singularity between the two sides. Somehow I doubted the outside world had been concealing it. That brought me to question how the house ended up having been built identically in both realities, especially since it was an 1897 Victorian; but stranger things had happened. My senses dictated that I narrow it down to a space inside it. I crisscrossed the entire place, including the attached garage, but to no avail. Nothing betrayed close proximity to the other side, no smell of exhaust fumes through a crack, not a faint sound of wailing sirens bleeding through a false wall—the house was mute. Finally, a bulb lit up—

the Governor had sat in the same corner of the room the two times I had come out of my blackouts, one in each house. He had also been there when I returned from my last hiking trip, before he took me back. It was easier to visualize, now that I had turned the living room into an office similar to the one in "A's world." I grabbed the chair used by the Governor, and positioned it in the very spot of my recollection of the time. I sat in it and closed my eyes.

— o —

I figured I must have nodded when I suddenly regained focus. I got up, my heart pounding, thinking I had crossed, but I was still home. I was both reassured and disappointed. I sat back in the chair, my elbows on my knees, a sense of partial defeat bearing on me. I finally got up, resigned to have to come up with plan B another time.

There was no plan B—I stood in the middle of the office, as a noisy motorcycle raced by the house. I ran to the garage; Little Honda was sleeping. I returned to the room, sat in the chair, and started to cry.

——— o ———

15 – ERASURE

Following the chocolate truffle and the crème brulée, John and I walk to the Ferris wheel. This time, I pay no attention to the lovers kissing on benches. I am preoccupied by what has been going on with him, but partially relieved he is finally opening up about his relation with the wife. Last week, he had admitted to having been used and emotionally abused—nothing like a true confession, even if only a small wave frisking around a wee beach rock. Now I need him to talk about the wife, tell me her real name, where she's from, the things she asked about, and most importantly, what she demanded of him in regard to the Program. I know he's not anxious to go deep, but he has to—time is no longer on his side.

From what I know, she was able to probe John the way she tried with me the one time I met her. I previously said that there was a chance she had done so, but as my story progresses, I feel less and less of a need to be reserved. Of course, the wife has drained John of all his fluids and is now in possession of what she coveted most from the beginning. I have already explained that the Program is not of the binary kind—it is the coalescence of all the energies that have joined it from the conceptual end. So, hoping to find a corrupt element within it is looking in the worst possible of places. She isn't inside it—nobody is—but she knows enough to now be part of it. In essence, she is in the process of replacing John.

Because the Program concerns itself with energy, it cannot distinguish between identities, and since there are too many of us around the world for anyone to notice a substitution, it is unlikely that the wife will get noticed. So, as I said before, that's when I come in, not just as an expert in extractive communication, but as an "overseer" as well. I joined that group after years of refining the art of "bridge-building." On a side note, one may say there is no-one left between the Governor and I.

The thing is, if it were for just the wife, there would not be much to worry about. After all, she would be facing powers incommensurably greater than hers, forces capable of sending her reeling to infinity and back. But she is not alone, and we do not know how many there are, where they are, who they hijacked, and when they plan on striking. Sadly, our only link is John, a drained man short on time.

— o —

Since I am a "bridge-builder," I can attest to the fact that even though we have bridges spanning the many streams that separate worlds, the winds of ill only come from "A's world". It isn't a fundamental evil as we imagine it, a force from the bowels of Hell; no, it is more like a contract on the Program by an organization that has all to gain from its demise—just think "fuel people" installing pumps all over our cities while junking our beautiful hydromobiles. In other words, they don't wish for their world to change, even in the face of imminent catastrophe. Thinking of it, that is pretty fiendish!

We have no business changing the course of destiny; if it is the choice of a race to self-obliterate, then so be it! But in the case of "A's" I am well placed to deduct it isn't a consensus. A majority wishes for positive change, not to mention that nature and its species would rather be thriving. The Program aims at restoring balance into willing worlds by guiding and advising those with the better voices, so when that wish is challenged by the bankrupt morality of a few, it engages the gears of investigative work at our end.

To be clear, we are not policy-makers; our job is not to enforce any rules. Nevertheless, we abide by our own guidelines, one of them specifically written to prevent unforeseen elements from corrupting the whole. As an example: we aim to help, so, if one day, one of our "tale-makers" changes the narrative in the subtlest of ways, we must be alerted immediately. If not, we could just as easily inflict damage. That is what happened with John when he sent corrupt data, thankfully, to an uncooperative "character."

— o —

So now, how do we proceed to prevent an agent of ill to infiltrate the "body positive" after they already have? That is, once again, how I end up being here. The way we bridge worlds, is also the way we bridge time; and the way we help worlds with healing, we must apply to our own. We know the corruption is already at work, and it is a matter of time before all unravels. We don't have armies to protect the Program, it was part of the design. My investigative work must take me back to a time point wherefrom I can make the necessary adjustments. Of course this present will be altered, but my dictation, being cyclic, will reflect the changes—it is my assignment to not lose the thread.

I must return to the early days of the bridge in order to search for what I missed then. Of course, I cannot

95

just be a passive observer of my own past—I must become the part, for there is no place for two active selves within one body. So, for the sakes of the Program and my world, I must cease to exist.

—— o ——

I'm still reeling from my first physical crossing. A moment ago, there was a distinct glitch—the experiment failed then succeeded. It succeeded when I had already accepted I had failed. I must look into it!

It feels good to cry when reality stops making sense. But what do I expect when I am responsible for it? At least, my reunification with my little auto friend is cheering my heart. I had missed her dearly.

But before I rejoice about my accomplishment, I'd better check how it works in reverse.

Since I am already sitting in the chair, I just close my eyes. There is a little flash in my mental vision and a slight snapping sound in the auratic field that I take as a sign that it's OK to open them again. Sure enough, I am back home. That's easy!

I shall stay here for a while, for I have no pressing need to rush into *A's world* unprepared. But then again, I have no clue as to what I should prepare for. My only possible connection with *A* is when I'm home. As I said before, I wouldn't know where to start to find him, plus, I don't think it's a good idea for the moment.

Now that the bridge is here, I need to figure out what to do with it. Obviously, I didn't build it just for the exercise—there is purpose that requires defining.

On my last trip, there was a list I worked from, whose results were to be incorporated into the Program, but I sense my experience took care of adding to the pool of knowledge—now we know how *A's world* split from us back in 1870. What we don't know is who was behind influencing the United States to join France against Prussia—I guess that's worth investigating. I mean, anyone that has the power to turn an entire civilization around away from the storm isn't just your regular person, and somehow I very much doubt it was an accident. So, there we have it, item number one—I know my calling when I hear it!

Of course, there are all the other things that need healing in that world. The problem is I cannot influence it beyond the inevitable ripples of my presence, by that I imply that it is against Program protocol to go past assisting consenting *characters*, which we do through *tale-making*. So, beyond reporting on my research, there isn't much I can think of for the time being. Naturally, I cannot count on the Governor to nudge me in the right direction.

— o —

For now, I feel rather numb emotionally. Actually, *feeling* is a big word in the absence of feeling; I doubt the bundled-up mess in my stomach qualifies. I even skipped one period because of the overload. I suppose that my idea of taking it easy doesn't fit the definition so well. I am too driven most of the time, and my one release is through the daily tears. In fact, I am perpetually on the edge of crying—sometimes out of joy, but mostly out of an indescribable sense of loss, some kind of disconnect from my love center. In spite of the noteworthy achievements, I can only feel the one half of me that deals with all things Program; the other belongs to my youth when John and I, and a few other friends lived carefree, metaphorically chasing butterflies all day long.

Talking of John, it would be nice to reconnect, even if the last I heard of him he was going through a dark phase. I had a crush on John—he was a vibrant teen with a sparkle in his eye and a keen intelligence. We kissed on one occasion but that was all he gave me. I don't think he was ever into me beyond play. I kept on keeping, as we say, but the rebuttal eventually eroded at my ability to hide how I felt to myself, and one day, I had grown beyond play. If it confused John to bear the rapid changes, he didn't show it. Instead he retreated to a reality that I would never be part of, and before long, we were off to college. One of these days, I'm going to check him out—just curious!

— o —

So, this is where I stand: with some practice, I can be in both Bayvilles whenever it suits me. I checked my bank account, my standing with DMV, and the rest of the paper trail that says I'm legit on *A*'s side, and all is in order. Interestingly enough, I own both houses with a different vehicle in each garage. It sort of amuses me that I should be in love with two machines, but that's the price to pay for not finding the time to be social and not having enough sex.

I am wondering at the side effects of not feeling connected to the larger body of the Program. I miss the students and the faculty, the sense of family and the stimulation that comes with having others around. I question my position as a lone she-wolf doing work for the greater collective. I do my best to imagine that I'm still attached to that whole in spite of the oddness of my particular settings, especially when, on one side, I am no longer in Program reality. But as the Governor always says, it is meant to be!

So far, all the important items play in my world—nothing on *A*'s side for the moment. Having the bridge will suffice in terms of stimulation. Actually, I have a guilty desire to take Little Honda for a ride tomorrow, so we're off to a good start!

— o —

After crossing the bridge, I decide to drive to South Bayland; S.B. 2, that is. During the ride, I ponder on the data I have been feeding *A*. I have a sense that he is taking it and saving it for later—I don't feel a book in the making. It doesn't matter to me at his point, everything is up in the air, as if sanity had left the picture—I feel somewhat schizophrenic.

My little friend purrs along the highway, taking me where my heart calls. The South Bayland 2 communities are a leftover mix of the 50s and 60s, two unlikely groups to ever get along: the loggers and the hippies. But somehow the gap has filled with the commonality of being outcasts of the system, one feeling abandoned by it, the other, wanting nothing to do with it. They realized their differences were only cosmetic.

— o —

In my usual fashion, I refrain from naming what isn't mine. *A's world* is not mine, and I refuse to compromise it. Let's just say that, on my side, the main South Bayland community is called Longville; I may call it L2, or not—I'm still refining the narrative.

As I mentioned on the drive, I'm not feeling myself. I have a sense that the Program is in fluctuation at a level I can't comprehend; a realignment perhaps. It's the oddest of sensations, like a switching of channels in my power center, if I may say.

I sit outside a café that serves bad coffee and dangerous pastries. I eat something that shouldn't have a name, but is given one anyway: doughnut. My mouth hates me. The owner's idea of a cup is a soft, white container made of small, round particles bound to each other—it's the strangest thing, and it too looks dangerous. I come here to relax; instead, I feel all tensed up from trying to act normally. The thing is that I don't know what normal is.

Sure, San Francisco 2 was a lot worse, but I could disappear in the crowd there. Here, it's as if all stretched out and slowed down to expose the minutest of non-conformity. In reality, only the eyes of a child are upon me, gazing at me as if trying to comprehend the woman behind the mask. I smile back at her. She looks at something above my head and then hops away—satisfied.

I sit here for the longest time, watching people walk by; the kind of people who have nothing to hide—it's how I know there is something hard in them. But aside from that, they are a lot like my people back home—definitely not like the big-city folks. I feel through them.

I did manage to convince the owner to serve me coffee in a proper cup, replacing the odd pastry, in the process, with the safety of a banana. I can now settle for a while. I am actually relaxing at last. Perhaps it was the child who reminded me that no purpose can be found in paranoia. *There's no rush, time is long*, she seemed to have said. Of course she's just being *her*, in her glorious state of existence. She is the essence of reason within a construct of madness by adults who don't know any better. What a strange place! But then, there is such bare honesty to that fundamental mistake, that I wonder if it's a mistake at all.

— o —

I still question why my heart wished to take me to Longville 2. I suspect it is because of nuances found in the unnatural marriage of elements that have lost their place in the world; a bit like the flowers from a cancelled wedding, no longer of importance, stripped of their purpose because of a glitch, a word misspoken, or a last-second change of mind. It doesn't take much.

I step out of my reverie—a native man seeks my attention. I'm not sure if he's sane, but he tells me that I should go home before darkness descends upon me; and then he chants in an old tongue. Oddly, it comes across more like advice than sinister forewarning. If I am correct, he knows what I already know. Some people can feel the direction of the wind better than others. All it takes is to water the roots of intuition every so often.

— o —

It's time for Little Honda to drive us back to the Bayville 2 house, and for me to re-cross the bridge. I have much to channel to *A* before I go to bed. For some reason, I feel it is important that he should know my story. Maybe one day, I might be able to understand the makings of my own mind. For now, I feel rather confused. But until then, I

102

want to enjoy the sight of the still-standing giants along the road, the beautification strip that gives the illusion the forest goes on for miles, but all there is to see beyond, is the ravage of clear-cutting. I pretend my world is overlapping like a big umbrella of hope.

— o —

I am back in my proper house, the one I bought with the saved money from my work as *Seven* in Rio and Adelaide. My name actually shows up on the title. I don't recollect signing any paperwork or making payments on the one in *A*'s, but, by some mysterious intervention, *she*'s all taken care for. Janette Trudy Smyth is also the title holder! I assume the Governor has something to do with it.

As promised, I connect with *A* and deliver the latest. I know he and I have an intimate relationship, but I am not sure of how that translates at his end. I wonder if he recognizes me as more than just the feminine side of his nature. But as we know, the brain is challenged by all things slippery. It would be so much simpler being two humans sitting across each other around cups of steaming coffee. So, beyond the improbability of reading *A*'s *work* in person, I don't really know what he does with the data. What I am sure of, at the heart level, is that he takes in the stuff—that's what matters! Until now, I had not realized what I was doing. My version of *tale-making* is very different from what was intended by the Program; for instance, *A* is not getting *a* story, but *my* story. I am not simply dictating to him, but sharing close, practically intimate details about my life and person. It came about that way because of reciprocated affinity for the man across that line between worlds. In a sense, he is my

103

sacred masculine. But these are also the early steps of *tale-making*, so may the subject be the test sample! To make it clear, I will advise against anything but fiction. I am a *designer* at the exploratory stage of possibilities. I'm only now understanding the dire repercussions of giving away our existence, for I suspect that it's just as conceivable to bridge from *A*'s side as it is from mine. Food for thought! But it is too late to reverse course as far as us two are concerned. It isn't really a risk at the level of just one *character*, and I'm sure *A* has no intentions of corrupting my world. If anything, based on his pain, he probably would want to be in it and stay.

— o —

As part of a comparative study, I've decided to visit San Francisco on both sides. I am on my way to the big city in my dad's well-cared-for present to me: the mighty hydromobile! It doesn't have a name, probably because it wasn't mine to start with, unlike Little Honda; and of course, it does not represent the sacred byproduct of close-up trauma, the unlikely saviour of the soul laid bare.

I have the roof down, my hair blowing in the wind. I rejoice at the fact I am actually relaxing, while taking in life in all of its splendour. The small road to the Bay Area, unlike the *freeways* of *A's world*, is the work of artistes. It is designed to make the trip an experience worth repeating. In fact, there are three of these roads, which at times cross each other in playful spans and underpasses. It doesn't escape me that my appreciation for the trip is made all the more vivid because of my knowledge of what is on the other side. It leads me to wonder how much we have lost in *sense intensity* from living in a near-perfect reality. But if I recall, there is no such awareness if comparisons cannot be made; what we take for granted is the very stuff of life, like the air we breathe—no need to fret about it.

— o —

San Francisco is a miracle of urban living. There are gardens on all of its tall roofs and terraces, trees everywhere; any reason to incorporate more of nature into its makeup is taken with unrestrained passion. Butterfly migration routes branch in myriad floral corridors teeming with unrelenting activity. There is an entire réseau of lanes, bridges, and tunnels that tie the numerous parks designed to support wild life. At the cost of repeating myself, the city is a miracle of co-habitation! Sure, allocated zones don't always prevent the elks from crossing the avenues, but we have a safety system that aims at protecting them from our transport machines.

I have my favourite places to visit, and a few friends from the Program I have not seen in a while. The Professor is joining me for a day of sightseeing, and I hope there is enough room for sex. Good stuff! But I am going there for studies! The aim is to isolate a few areas, analyze behavioural patterns within them, and select various artifacts of historic and cultural value to use as background. Then the same gets repeated on the other side. In the end, I must come up with a synthesis of the two in the form of a comprehensive report. To be clear, I wasn't asked to do it. Remember, I was both student and teacher in Straßburg, so self-assigning is in my court, especially in the capacity of *designer* specialized in fringe

105

experiments. Enough said for now—I'm off to visit with friends!

— o —

I didn't expect a party with the presence of Alice and Max from my Monterey days. Too bad the Professor isn't coming until tomorrow! The hosts are past co-students, so, naturally, there are many familiar faces. It is protocol to not discuss anything-Program between us during private gatherings, and it's no exception here; although, we are free to explore where we're at in our relation to it, like such and such is now teaching at such at such Chapter. Mind you, I am recalcitrant to talk about my post, so I don't mention *designing*. For all they know, I'm on a leave of absence to concentrate on putting order to my studies—not a total lie.

We are at the peak of the brouhaha when I notice a very familiar face across the room—John's. The surprise makes my heart jump. He is accompanied by a tall woman wrapped in the kind of clothes that hide little of her shapes. Rather than walking to him, I decide to wait and see if he recognizes me. I catch his gaze, but save for a brief hesitation, he stays focused on his entourage. It's a fact that we have changed; after all, we haven't seen each other in over a decade, so there is no need interrupting a conversation for the sake of stirring the past; the party will go on for a while.

So, I return to my group, asking about the life in San Francisco, plans, expectations, kids; the in-passing questions about pain and happiness, playacting close ties for a chance to share such things—what we do at parties! I refrain from alcohol. Mind you, alcohol isn't the universal choice for recreational substances—Bayland Green is. Out of the blue, it makes me realize that hippies happened in both *A* and my world—something to look closely into.

By the time I return to John, he's gone, and so is his attention-seeking companion. I take it I have missed my opportunity. I really wanted to see him again—oh well!

I wish the Professor were here, since Max and Alice have apparently been hijacked by a group of younger students. I guess the same patterns keep on looping in Monterey. Good for them! Honestly, it bothers me somewhat. It's just that we were so close then; sharing a bed with the older generation was a high that I had made personal—a kind of ownership. It's amazing what we store and never deal with. So, in other words, I feel partially abandoned; *me*, the high-ranking kamikaze *designer*, experimental bridges et al.

While I wallow in fake misery, John reenters the picture, alone. I consider my chances—I go for it. For a second, he looks at me with a blank stare, and then, finally, *Janette!* It's nice not to be totally forgotten. We hug each other. I learn—for the second time—that he joined the Program a year after me. For now, he teaches in Buenos Aires, where he met his wife. He is professor twenty-four, *Twenty-Four* for short. My telling of me being *Seven* seems to confound him. *You're first generation; how is that possible!?* he exclaims. How do I respond to that? Well, I tell him that graduating with top honours in all subjects and Chapters propelled me to the post. Based on his reaction, I refrain from elaborating, for there is something that rankles of competition in his demeanour that puts me on the defensive. I didn't expect that from him, and now that I have refocused my receptors, I see that he's not the same person I knew. I am having a hard time imagining that the Program could have radicalized him, but I think I'm in the neighbourhood of the truth—if not the Program then something else—another item to add to the list!

— o —

My brief meeting with John took us back to our teens, but the era after it is protected by something I am not in the capacity of describing yet. It is void-like, unreachable, forbidden. I opted not to probe, draw attention to myself. We promised to stay in touch; perhaps we will. Finally, I get Alice and Max to myself. We reminisce about the times shared, though the adventurous stuff isn't mentioned, which I find sad in a kind of resigned way. People change.

I cannot say that my reintroduction to the old crowd distinguishes itself by its surplus of joy and honesty, for I find the party fit for a sigh, but I'm here on a journey of the personal, for the sake of not only the Program, but of comprehending the changes within me. Perhaps my contact with *deceit* is hardening me; meaning *A's world* is weighing on my person.

At this point, I'm not sure I want to see the Professor, but I am not quite ready to leave San Francisco yet. Maybe we'll rain-check and I'll tour the city by myself. I call his number.

— o —

It's probably a good thing the Professor didn't get my call, for we are presently having a fine time being out

108

on the town. I spent the night at a bed and breakfast in the Haight. The Professor called early to let me know he was in the city. As it turned out, his phone was out when I tried him. It must have been meant to be that way. We had breakfast at a busy place, enjoyed the food, played footsies, and most importantly, laughed. So, now I know there's nothing wrong with me—hardness has not yet ruined inner joy. The thought goes well with the laughter that still rings within us as we sit on a bench, lazily watching passersby. I tell him about my chance encounter with my old friend John. He knows John from having taught him at the Monterey Chapter. Without me probing, the Professor lets me in on the fact John was on his radar on numerous occasions. He mentions distinct disconnects, not from a lack of interest, but from something that arose out of disagreement. It didn't happen often enough to raise a major concern—it was understood that young minds had to flex their new powers on and off—but John's intensity was close to being off the charts. I ask what he means by that. His answer: *I considered bringing the issue to the faculty, but in the end, I rescinded out of fairness—the Program needed new blood, so, what was wrong with a bit of hot-headedness? It wasn't like John was adamant about his views; it wasn't even about views, just a reflexive attitude that belonged to the young with a small chip on their shoulder!* I don't necessarily agree with the diagnosis; what I saw last night was a lot more than an attitude; it was aggressive, and at the same time, hidden. The Professor looks at me without saying anything. I sense he is curious, but refrains, but then he asks, *What are you up to Janette?* I cannot let him in on the latest accomplishments, but I can't hide the fact that I have recently been drawn to seeing John again; something that rarely has crossed my mind in the last decade. Yes, during that time, I wished to know how he did, but on only two occasions: when I visited Junction Station between Chapters. Beyond that, he was never in my thoughts. The Professor is satisfied with my answer.

OK, what the Hell, I might as well relax one of my cardinal rules; after all, he hasn't been the best kept secret: the Prof's name is Chance, Chance Isca. It was becoming tedious to conceal the identity of such a ubiquitous character—unlike the Governor whose name has never been told. At any rate, it's Chance from now on! I know; I could coerce *A* into doing some editing, but I prefer staying on the side of unpredictability; it suits the beat of the artistic heart.

— o —

I'm heading north. Chance and I spent the night at a motel by the beach; it was fabulous—my body thanks me! So now, it's the same in reverse, hair to the wind, a beautiful drive all the way home! As I pass Longville, I wonder how the native man and the child are doing on the other side. Somehow, a part of me is still there.

——— o ———

17 – REPORT № 1

It's seven, time to get up! The first thing I did, last night, was update *A* on my trip to San Francisco. Still no idea what happens to the dictation, but I trust it is what it is. I go over my notes, the high points and the low ones. It all is a bit muddled by the fog in my mind. Coffee kicks in and I feel the urge to check on the other side. The thought occurs that doing so is like taking the refuse to the curb for pick-up—another thing to cross off the list of daily chores. Little Honda is in the garage waiting for her turn to take me to *San Francisco*.

Alright, from now on, I shall italicize all the places in *A's world* that share names with mine, like I just did above with San Francisco. Starting immediately, Bayville 2 is now *Bayville*, Longville 2: *Longville*, Junction Station 2: *Junction Station*. You get the drift! I think it will simplify the narrative. It's not like *A* asked, but I am perceiving intermittent hesitancy at his end. Call it intuition. Remember that he thinks—at least I believe he does—that I am his sacred feminine, hence a part of him. It's probably just the junior editor in him knocking at my door. But I have to be honest, when it comes to *A*, I am put to the test. At times, I doubt that he is more than a figment of my imagination. It's a vulnerability, for sure, but who doesn't have a moment of uncertainty on occasion? At least I have *the bridge* to prove that I'm not totally insane. I created it out of a sense of purpose, the intention to connect with the reality of *A's*, to aid his world recover from abuse. That isn't the dream of a mad woman, or is it? But all existential crises aside, I'm glad to find my little auto friend in its corner. All is well! I check the air outside, gauge the noise level; all that to make sure dream and reality aren't intermingling. I promise myself to make it a routine, even if I have no business to conduct across *the bridge*. (Note to self and *A*: keep on italicizing 'the bridge.')

— o —

The high point of my San Francisco visit was meeting with Chance; the low one: the party and my bumping into John. Funny how that went; I wanted to see John and almost canceled my date with Chance. Am I that out of synch with my environment, or is the influence of *A's world* turning the tables around? Keeping a foot grounded is of the essence here! I take note of the detail.

OK, focus, Janette!

The high point needs no extrapolating—I feel complete. As to the low one, and putting John to the side, the party was dulled by dull people and their dulled out lives; a sad state of affair among the brilliant few. It must have been an off-day. But let's go a bit deeper: my personal mood wasn't any cheerier than that of the gathering—ha!

It is clear; it started with my awareness of John and his wife in the room, culminating in my sense of disbelieve about how much he had changed inside. Right there is our theoretical villain—the dullness came with John. Yet, he was far from dull himself, the way I recall our interaction. And then, there is his wife, *the wife*, if I may, who stood at serious odds with the party. I mean, we are Pacific Coasters, the exemplification of casual; then shows up this decked-out gal—a vortex for attention—

112

who displays her form in a direct mockery of what we stand for: authenticity. Which one of the two was the chill in the room, John or his wife, the model?

I know I am onto something important; it rings in my bones. I wonder how Chance would have acted had he showed up—I need reference here! Back to the time of my arrival: people appeared cheerful and engaging—fact! The apex of the party precisely preceded John and *the wife*'s entrance—fact! The saying, *If it looks like a duck, swims like a duck...* sits square with my frame of mind. The dullness that enrobed the gathering was the result of energy being sucked out of the room, vibrancy replaced by exactly its opposite: lassitude. Everything went back to normal the minute I returned to the Bed and Breakfast— the Haight was bouncing!

— o —

Writing the report puts me in touch with my inner self. The feeling that arose from within at the party is precisely what I need to focus on, since it is likely the place where the things that are meant to remain invisible, end up resting. Let's face it; I very much doubt any of the party-goers pondered about the quality of their moods for too long, if at all. Again, it's my job to see the unseen, and why I should be the one hopping *bridges*. For now, I feel more like an investigator than a *designer*. I also feel a new wind has shifted the direction of my personal weather vane. And that, my friends, is where it gets truly eerie for this girl!

I have no doubt the Governor set me up for yet another of his mysterious assignments that only makes sense towards completion. But every time, it gets more

113

complicated, obscure, and lonely. I cannot fight my willingness to go along; no-one forced me to work on refining *tale-making*, and no-one could have prevented me from building *the bridge*. I recognize the Governor is only the punching bag for my occasional discontentment with the self. If I had never met him in person, I wouldn't shy away from the conclusion that he's just a metaphor for the emergence of personal powers in the face of old fears. But I have known him to be real, so there!

— o —

In those depths of mine lie the many knowns turned unknowns. Fortunately, I don't have to scrape the bottom with my own nails yet. Rather, what I'm looking for is what stirred the murky waters—a mere probing for what lurks below the surface will suffice.

For a force to take away the radiance of a room filled with Program people, speaks of power. To do it with stealth, speaks of purpose. Now, I have a hard time imagining that power and purpose in the same room is purely accidental, and that it is the work of a single individual on an ego trip. Purpose in that setting is suspicious of Program affiliation, and not necessarily for the benefit of it. It seemed like a test, an experiment, and sadly, a successful one. I need to contact the Governor.

— o —

He is always easy on me, the Governor; he shows up when either I'm done with a job or when something important needs his participation. Now that he's here, I know it's important!

114

I go over my notes and conclusions with him, and though he focuses on my points, I have a sense it isn't news to him—nothing is *ever* news to him! For the first time, I muster the strength to share my observation. He smiles as if he had been waiting for that moment. He tells me that *bridge-building* would eventually answer my greater questions about him, and that I am, from now on, in charge of its program. As to the *now*, all he is aware of are possibilities; though he implies that by *awareness*, he means a quality I would soon enough discover for myself, a moment he deems deserving of a surprise that needs not be spoiled. How is that for clarification! On the other hand, the Program is giving my research carte blanche, which translates as: not only is it important that I continue, but the results will determine the course of things to come; in other words, we're facing trouble. I congratulate my intuitions.

— o —

My meeting with the Governor turns out to be another bag of mixed feelings. He knows, yet he doesn't know; he guides, yet he lets the guidance take care of itself. It's more like he suggests, refines by evasion, pulls assignments like hares out of a hat, saying, *Voilà, we're done!* It is as if time didn't seem to affect him. Nonetheless, he's gone before I have a chance to figure out how he does it. Same chair as when I cross *the bridge*—different destination. What about that for another detail to add to the list!

Well, carte blanche says it all; I have my work cut out. Next is my trip to *San Francisco* in Little Honda. I'd better get prepared with an agenda I can pit against the

115

first report, even if in the end it proves unnecessary. While the first trip was exciting in a joyful way, this one comes with anxiety. But I find comforting humour in thinking of myself as a strange woman in a strange land. There is a ring of wicked complicity to it.

——— o ———

18 – REPORT № 2

Once more, I stop in *Longville*. I sit at the same table, my coffee in a proper mug, and a serving of mildly dangerous vanilla pudding with a glowing red cherry on top. I forego the cherry, which looks highly suspicious, and settle into my two-step routine. I don't know what I am expecting, but *Longville* seems like the right place for a pit stop. Of course, the child is nowhere in sight and the tribal man, though he is around, doesn't seem to recognize me. It's just as well; I'm not in a mood for a doomsday announcement, although, to be perfectly honest, part of me longs for one. After all, I am investigating, so any message is good omen, even in the shape of a bad one.

Last night, as customary, I handed all I had to *A*, who responded with his usual appreciative kindness. I can't say enough how much I love the man.

I was quite nervous, this morning, when I took Little Honda out of the garage for her *fuel breakfast* at the local pump. It's not like she is feisty—to the contrary—in fact, she's rather easy to drive. No, I mean, the other autos always scare me, until I collect my nerves. So much aggressivity, intermixed with utterly selfish heedlessness, makes me wonder how *A's world* manages to find its order—it's extraordinary! The same thing in mine would send the collective makeup into chaos.

I got out of town, happy to see cows minding their own business. I admire the stoicism of cows, a Zen defense of sort, I understand. In my world, they are a lot more engaging and playful though. But it's a long story.

The freeway is quite lovely from south of *Bayville* all the way to *Santa Rosa*; after that it's complete madness. But I'm still in *Longville* enjoying my pudding, trying my best to put on an easygoing exterior over bundled nerves, which in a funny way, aligns me with the locals—easygoing with an uneasy edge. After a while I take off, resigned to my fate. I don't know anyone in *San Francisco*, but I have booked a room in a motel by the long beach, in the same area Chance and I stayed, but a block south. The Pacific looks the same in both worlds, but I know that below its waters, stories play on a different theme. It was part of my research when the Governor brought me across *his bridge* into here.

Getting into *San Francisco* was a tedium I wish not to repeat. Little Honda started to overheat up the *Waldo Grade*, and I thought she wasn't going to make it. I'm glad to be safe on the beach, watching the sunset; I can relax now—well, almost—the tears are coming out, released from deep strata. I sit on the wet sand, returning to the waters what belongs to the sea, the tears and the menstrual blood. When it rains, it pours!

— o —

After a greasy breakfast at a local diner, I decide to put my thoughts in order. Little Honda will remain in the auto park of the motel while I check the city. Based on my last experience with her here, she is relieved by my choice. Instead I shall call one of the bully yellow taxis that wreak havoc in the downtown section. It you can't fight them, join them! I read the quote in a silly book—I like it! The taxi driver picks me up; it's only seven. After he asks, *Where to?* he drives us smoothly eastbound on

118

one of the big boulevards. I like his composure, precise, but not too rushed. There is an air about him that feels of the familiar, but there's no reason for it. After a while, I notice something is making him uncomfortable. I ask if he's OK—he replies by asking me if we have met before. Something is odd here, but I keep it to myself. *What do you do?* I probe. He's a musician in a rock band, a lead guitarist and composer. I ask him if he writes. He sort of does; he has ideas he would like to put on paper, but he's still working on his English. He wants to do it right, maybe later in life. *What kind of writing?* I feel abruptly curious—it couldn't be!? *Fiction, metaphysics, a merging of the two...* I hear. He asks for my name. *Janette? C'est parfait !* he exclaims. His is on the dashboard ID, which, oddly, would be coming handy if I knew *A's*—I draw a pathetic blank. He is in a relationship, but something came down he prefers to not elaborate on. I'm glad he chooses it that way; I don't like the *poor me* sobbing of hypocrisy. I'm all ears when he says, *Hey, I created the mess; I'll figure it out!* My kind of man! I might as well ask him where he stands on women; it's always a good litmus test of male integrity. He surprises me there—his answer: *Give me a good reason to love men!* That shuts me up. I think I know where he is coming from—I sense he means it.

It's a long fare to downtown, but not long enough to get what I need to know about him. I propose that he show me the city—I'm new here, and what better way to do it than in a taxi, at the mercy of someone who has explored all of its crannies? At the next stoplight, he turns around, somewhat suspicious; but then we are looking each other in the eyes, and I feel my heart jumping around like a mad pony. I hand him a hundred dollar bill, asking if he wants more—I don't care how much it costs. He relaxes. *Don't worry; I'll take care of you. You pay me later*, he says, returning the money. But there's a shake in his voice—something has crumbled way deep; I just sense it! Do we know each other? Hell yes! Except, let's be real, how can we!? I think of *A*, but I don't want to think of *A*. It's the worst place to think of him, inside a box, at the mercy of my deepest hopes and fears. Oh my, I'm going to faint. I think about the Program, while he negotiates his way around a particularly tricky obstacle, something to cool the heat, the out-of-control arousal. If he feels a fraction of what churns inside me, he exhibits unusual countenance. I guess it is his job to put the shields up when danger lurks. I am danger breathing down his neck. But then he turns around again, putting on an irresistible smile: *You're beautiful, really, I mean it— no strings attached!* How do you respond to that when you're approaching meltdown!? I mean, my God—have mercy! *Thank you!* that's all I say; just like that—cold and surgical. Did I beg to spend the next couple of hours in the presence of this man? Humor to self: I create my own reality, I'll figure it out! *You're welcome!* He's killing me. I want him to be *A*! He's not! I want him to be *A,* regardless! It's not like I can ask him. He's attractive and I'm beautiful, and we both mean it; why can't we just do something with it? Let's just fuck and get it over with! But it's not in the contract—it's not happening. He has a bad girlfriend, a child on the way, maybe another lover on the side; give the man a break! That cools me off; it's about time—I'll masturbate later.

With that, we drive around, and at noon, we take a break at a taco joint on Haight Street. For a stranger, I find him rather engaging, this man should go places. He tells me that a couple of years prior, he worked close to the French president as one of his communication crew. I guess he already went places. Strange he would now be driving taxis though; maybe it's a lie. He also tells me that he wasted many opportunities in rock and roll. I sense he has regrets about it. All I come up with is that opportunities are always in the making. He agrees.

Before we take off for the second half of the sightseeing programme, a tall woman, in a colourful outfit, enters the taqueria. I know her from somewhere, make that: I feel *her* from somewhere. And then, it hits me like a tidal wave—*the wife*, John's wife from supposedly Buenos Aires, now in the *San Francisco* of *A's world*! I rest my case, we have collusion! Forget the hots for the driver; I am getting blowtorched by some nasty winds! We'd better get out of here before she smells me; now isn't the time to give the game away, especially right at its start.

Fair enough, we are out of trouble's way before trouble awakens. My crush of the morning, turned Mister Safe, takes me around in his magic yellow mobile. I am presently relaxing, with an artiste at the wheel, colouring the town in a voice of French-accented tones. He probably doesn't know who I am, but I know who he is, plus I have his number. As to me, I use payphones.

I could be wrong about him though.

— o —

We stop in *Willits*. I had noticed the small vegetable market on the way down, promising myself to investigate upon return. I was not aware of the term *organic* until now. I get it: without chemical poisons. The place also sells raw-milk cheese sandwiches and real fruit drinks. I have a new regular pit stop; sorry *Longville*!

Little Honda and I left early in the morning; early enough to miss traffic madness. I am finally getting around! Starting mid-span on the Golden Gate, which incidentally is a better-looking bridge than ours, I have been going over what happened *yesterday*. After the taxi driver dropped me off at the motel, I lay on my bed looking straight at the ceiling. I needed a blank space to organize my thoughts. I didn't expect to bump into what I had been looking for, without knowing what it was, and with such speed. I go out and bam! here come *A* and *the wife*! Though, I must exercise caution with *A*; I could be in deep trouble projecting. It didn't stop me from masturbating like I promised myself—I could use all the release in the world!

The thing is, *the wife*'s presence here in *A's world* is particularly unsettling. What is her business in *San Francisco*, plus, aren't I supposed to be the first, besides the Governor, with a *bridge* to this side? That pretty much firms up my suspicion that *mine* is not the only one to span our realities. A sense of having been robbed of intellectual property looms over my head. I am in charge of the *bridge program*, me, the *designer*; so why wasn't I informed by the Gov of the possibility of a pre-existence of crossways—or was I? Now, I think of the chair in my office that serves dual purpose—where does it take him? OK, I get it: I may be the first *bridge-builder* in the Program, but others have preceded me elsewhere, and perhaps, by as much as history itself. In that case, why am I investigating foul play? Could it be that John is onto something that has purposely been kept away from me? It's somewhat out of character for the Program or the

Governor to stage something that wicked... No, I am still in charge, and the reason why no other can do my job, is because I am the only one capable of meeting the challenge. I take a bite out of my sandwich.

— o —

The point is to determine which side *the wife* belongs to, before speculating on her reasons to seek proximity of the Program. For that, I may have to keep my connection with John. The idea of going to Buenos Aires on the other hand doesn't excite me. I am also very intent on finding which other exits might live at the end of *my bridge*; for I am beginning to suspect multiple realities may be involved. But the scope of that concept takes my mind into an out-of-control whirl. I don't think I can go there! The thought retracts as quickly as it emerged. Simplify, Janette!

So, after checking Little Honda's oil and coolant, we left *San Francisco* as the sun rose to stretch its long, straight amber fingers amid the shadows of hills, trees, and houses. We followed the ocean along the beach, and then the rugged coast, until we came to the Golden Gate. I began thinking of *A* in a cross-pattern of thinking about *the wife*. It was *A*, it wasn't *A*; it was *A*, et cetera, et cetera. I remember what was said upon my first crossing: *Do not try to locate your 'character'!* Well, I didn't try to locate *A*, did I? So, if *A* throws himself at me, what am I supposed to do? The churning went on and on. In the end, I decided that whether it was *A* or not who drove me around, the point was elsewhere. He was the one, after all, who made it possible for me to bump into *the wife*, in a place she either belonged to or not—same difference.

123

Only *that* man, with his influence on me, could have made me want to be driven around until we opted for lunch at the taqueria. Synchronicity is the name of the game! So who's the man, may I ask? He surely had me in trouble for a minute, and that is not in my character to loose it so easily. One way or the other, meeting him was absolutely necessary and incontestably meant to be; I shall not renege on the statement.

— o —

Okay, now we have a suspect and an ally; one who seems to have a free pass in crossing worlds, the other that exists physically in one, and who may be accessible from the other via a form of deep exploration of the self, called *tale-making*. That, friends, is as wicked as it gets—not to mention working on intuition from inside a case with no name! All I have is a suspicion of foul play regarding the Program, which involves an old friend and his wife. In other words: nothing! Now, I can look at myself in the mirror and ask what in the world is happening to me. Time to hit the road!

— o —

I'm wailing; solitude is getting to me. I need a friend on this side, in *Bayville*. My *San Francisco* crush is out of question—his job is done! I will meet with *A* in person when the time is right. Anyway, I said a friend, not someone whose arms I want to die in.

Incidentally, we pass *Longville*, we don't pull over. I have a new favourite stop with better coffee and food without the chemical poisons—organic, baby!

We arrive *home* in the late afternoon. My Little mechanical friend is tired. I shall take her to a special place to have her looked over. Maybe she needs the kind of love I am incapable of providing. I too am exhausted, physically, emotionally, and mentally. Lots of reflecting, analyzing, dissecting to the point of confusion. Too much thinking about the inner process can't be healthy, can it? But here we are again!

OK, first thing first, I must connect with *A*. For that, I need to cross *the bridge*. Hell, I had planned on staying in *Bayville* for a couple of days to reacquaint myself with its beat. Did the Governor know I would turn into a lunatic!? He probably did, the bastard! I have no other choice; Bayville, here I come!

———— o ————

19 – MORE BRIDGES

A week has passed since my crazy visit to *San Francisco*. I walked around *Bayville* a few times in quest of a friend, but unlike the things that are meant to be, that friend is obviously not one of them. For the sake of peace and quietude, I opt to spend most of my private time in my Bayville, or visit with my parents in Junction Station. But, to be honest, there's a part of me that longs for the danger of the other side. *Bayville* has become the host of some incomprehensible guilty pleasure. I'm having a sense of not being entirely whole without a bit of both in my blood. Nonetheless, most of my work is done at home. By work, I mean the case I am working on. It's now a case; I've made it official! Short of coming up with solid data, I have decided to factualize my experience so that it fits my suspicions of wrongdoing on the part of John, his wife, and most likely, others. I'm alone, so what stops me from supporting my inklings with a semblance of structure. I felt the unlikely chill at the party, John and his wife happened to be there, and then *the wife* shows up in *A*'s *San Francisco*. That is legit enough material for me to take off from. Carte blanche is carte blanche—I can only be right!

Now that I've gotten this off my chest, I can ground and become me again. It's a tough wish because I've not been myself for quite a while. In fact, I feel like I'm about to explode out of my boundaries, as if more of me occupied a fixed space. It's an uncanny sensation that is as unsettling as it is mesmerizing—a lot like a hormonal charge racing through my befuddled self, funneling the carrier winds of memories I don't possess. I know there is foul play with John, but I cannot stir the nature of my discomfort to the open. I imagine *the wife* is serious trouble, but besides her crossing, I am incapable of pointing to where that trouble may be. That being said, and above all: I must heed my intuitions and grow the spine to support them—a steel spine.

Paradoxically, my one connection in *A's world* is the *San Francisco* taxi driver. I have chosen to treat the two, him and *A*, as separate beings in spite of my inklings. There is purpose to it based on logic. To enforce the paradox, *A* exists in relation to my reality, while the driver doesn't. I have to live with the irony that even if they are the same, they cannot be. So now, I am free to call the cabbie on a date; and to hell with the mess he has made of his life—if he likes danger, let him meet danger!

— o —

My call is received by a giggly woman, apparently high on weed, who tells me my friend is somewhere dealing with *hard shit*. I ask what kind of hard shit, and as it turns out, his girlfriend has raided his studio, destroyed his art, master tapes, photos, and various equipment with knives, or razor blades, leaving blood all over. She doesn't have a number for me to reach him at, thus advises to call again when the shit settles. Did I say, *To hell with the mess he has made of his life!*? Oh Man, here we go again, the grand prize for irony! I worry myself sick about all the data in *A's* possession. One irrational move and it's the end of my brainchild, the end of *tale-making*, my main contribution to the Program, the reason for my *designer* status and why I am presently in charge

127

of *bridge-building*. I race back to my Bayville to connect with *A* before the irreparable happens.

A's in trouble; his energy is all over the map. All I can do is soothe him, bathe him in love, for I sense he's about to commit the unthinkable. I can read his bleeding rage, the incommensurable injustice inflicted upon him, the fundamental rape tearing through his being; it's awful! The pain, so much pain, and so much fury surrounding him! I scream across the shield, *Come back, I love you, I need you—we all need you!* Then, all stops. It's not a mortal kind of silence, but a regular one made more silent by the forces standing at its gates. A frame frozen in time, a split second turned eternity. The suspense collapses as the storm moves away. I sense release. I believe the worst has been averted.

Well, so much for being unsure about *A* and the taxi driver—it's all clear now. I call the giggly woman back. She asks me if I want to speak with *A*. *No, thank you, I just want to know if he's alright.* —*Close call,* she says, *we all thought he had killed that witch with the kitchen knife. Good thing he had a change of heart! — Thanks, I'll try again when things settle!* I hang up.

— o —

Now that it's clear *A's* the driver, I must keep my distance. Since no mention was made of any destroyed writing, he and I shall simply revert to our soul meetings. It's obvious that my reckless impulses are not factored into our rapport. I must, from now on, concentrate on John, which means I shall remain in my world for a while. I've also decided to inform Chance of my doings— I need help from someone I can trust.

The Prof and I arrange for another meeting in San Francisco. I haven't told him yet about my case; I want to wait until we are face to face. Too much is lost in translation when latency and a lack of body language impose restrictions on communication. I have taught that the clearest path to truth is the shortest one: a table's width between two sets of eyes.

— o —

I normally never take the road through my Willits, but this time I make an exception. No disappointment there, the town's adorable! The food, well, it is of course delicious and one hundred percent *organic*! We don't have such a term here—it has no reason to exist. We don't consider poison an item that belongs to food. Food is medicine, nothing to remotely desecrate with vileness. I don't know what's wrong with *A's world*; I mean, I see what is wrong, but I can't see for the life of me what made it that way. So many lies! Anyway, I need to keep that reality from my thoughts for the time being. God knows how much I will have to spend there locating the villains in the dark alleys of my case.

I sit at one of the tables outside the market, watching people showing love for each other. They don't need the extreme of pain to appreciate what they have; that is another construct, another lie, a misplaced item of philosophy that only belongs across *the bridge*. But it takes one to have been there to recognize when a breach has been made. The San Francisco party was the site of such an event. For a whole hour, *A's world* bled through, and it will bleed through again at the hands of those who want to see the Program fail. Unless someone stops them before the shield gives under the pressures. Here comes the cavalry!

— o —

Chance and I meet at our regular place, regular starting today. Right away, I tell him the whole story. *A* fascinates him, but knowing the professor has a kink for threesomes, he certainly isn't thinking about *tale-making*. But there is no doubt his focus regroups when the subject of *the chill* and its perpetrators comes into frame.

To my surprise, I am not the only one, outside the Governor, who has suspected that the Program exposed serious vulnerabilities. But unlike me who's been in *A's world* to understand the possible harm such energy could inflict, Chance has no such reference, yet he's aware of something, as hypothetical as it may be. I am relieved by the reception; for one second, I feared that my work would be regarded as too fringe for consideration. Chance isn't just interested, he insists on joining me in the investigation. I ask him about the Monterey teaching job, only to learn that, just like me a couple of years ago, he has been put on rest leave by the Governor. How coincidental!

Of course, *rest leave* stands for educational leave, or more precisely, *do what you wish as long as it benefits the Program*. Technically, both of us are now on rest leave, and I assume it comes with carte blanche. Don't tell me this wasn't meant to be!

Now that Chance and I are on the same page and agree that John and *the wife* are up to something, comes the time to make a plan. Logic dictates that we meet before the two return to Buenos Aires, but we both

130

acknowledge logic may not be the best way to go at it—
that would be falling into something they might expect.
After all, Chance was John's teacher; an untimely interest
in their persons might be all they need to intuit their game
is up, which means ours is too. An accidental encounter
must be arranged. As it turns out, one of the students is
throwing a party in Monterey, which might conveniently
include John and *the wife*. Chance is working on it. As to
my presence there, well, I'll technically be on vacation.

— o —

As Chance and I talk about *the bridge*, he suggests
the possibility others could be built in various places.
Why limit the crossing to one lowly chair in my home,
especially one that is being used to access other places,
when there could just as well be other spots willing to
offer their unique services? And why not start with here,
the motel, an ideal meeting ground?

And so, after having explained to Chance the
rudimental method by which I travel between worlds, the
two of us embark on a joined meditation while sitting at
the foot of the bed. With nary an expectation, the little
brain crackle/flash that accompanies success is felt—we
open our eyes onto the very room I stayed in on my last
visit to *A's San Francisco*, a block away! *Whoa, Janette!*

— o —

Alarmingly, we haven't just crossed; we have also
landed in the closest approximation of our point of
departure. In my rush to get things going, I used the motel
as a target point, while foregoing the knowledge that the

one in *A's world* was a block south of us. It was reckless! Big lesson in *bridge-building*: select your destination carefully! We look around, and not surprisingly, the room is already in use. Luckily for us, the occupants are out. We reverse course, counting our blessings.

— o —

Because our world and *A*'s share a common history, the assumed safest candidates for *bridge points* are the buildings that existed prior to the split. It, of course, limits our options in countries such as the Amerikas, but offers unimaginable potential in old Europa, say. But then, I think about the ravages of two World Wars. Best is to research before striking—a job that shouldn't require too much time and energy if reduced to the creation of a short list of locations. As our next exercise, we try the beach, and sure enough, we land on the beach. But rather than return to our reality, with the help of the credit card I use in *A's world*, we book a room at the sleazy motel a block away from ours, and proceed with creating a safe *bridge* between the two. It works like magic, especially when we find ourselves back in our room. Now, we have a bed on both sides! How it works is mostly contingent on how far we are in the Program, and how much accumulated knowledge is acting in our favour. Chance and I are First-Generation, and that counts for something!

So, now we have a means to build *bridges* wherever we need them. The next logical step is to link them. For example, if from *Bayville* I were to book a room at the sleazy motel, I would want to be able to bridge it from my office in the Bayville of my world; get it? Another one of Chance's brainstorms! Proper mapping is paramount and we get on it immediately. The main points of connect, as far as the case is concerned, are Bayville, San Francisco, Monterey, and Buenos Aires on our side, and then *Bayville, San Francisco, et cetera* on the other. All these points should be accessible from each other; that's the plan! To make it happen safely, we must first search for places that exist in both realities in the year 1986. Bayville/*Bayville* is a no-brainer. The two motels in both San Francisco's are set. Next come Monterey and Buenos Aires.

— o —

On our way south, Chance and I further brainstorm on *bridge-charting*. From Monterey, we hope to establish linkage with San Francisco and Bayville—that's why we have booked rooms for a week at the two motels. After some minor debating, we settle on exploring the area of the San Carlos Cathedral for a potentially safe site. If proven suitable enough, we can then define and collect our necessary markers. Providing all works out as planned, we should be able to secure a third solid position, and perchance, find the means to cross-hop from one place to another.

Upon getting to Chance's place late in the day, we learn that the party isn't happening due to last minute cancellations, including those from John and *the wife*. In the absence of socializing, we opt to walk to the cathedral instead. Night crossing seems a solid option, using the Prof's house as departure point, and the cathedral proper for arrival. We take a mental picture of the ideal landing spot for the experiment, and then return to the house to freshen up and put some dinner together.

133

Chance's place looks the same as I last saw it; clean, but loose enough to bring a funk element to the decor. I adore his pad; it's like a second home to me, one I haven't seen in ages but whose welcoming warmth says, *I remember you!* It might remember the cry of lovers, the smell of sweaty bodies rocking in the heat of passion, the laughter amid the clinging of glasses... I, on the other hand, remember how it kept us safe.

— o —

At midnight, we take our positions. The mental picture is now part of the larger frame of our beings; it is the nave in which we stand with our eyes closed; it is also the nave in which we stand when we open them.

Success is sweet when it rolls like a dance. It's a tango, it's a waltz; we walk the aisle under a shower of roses. We've got it down! It no longer is approximate; it is controlled, it's surgical. All we needed were the two of us, trusted friends and lovers—I am elated! And so is Chance. Precise markers are the name of the game—we can be anywhere we choose from anywhere we stand, no need for chairs, *bridges* are everywhere!

We return to the house, convinced we have reached a major milestone. This is so good for the Program—such advancement—*bridge-building* is here to stay! I know there could be a downside to it, but I don't care for now, and neither does the Prof; he too is in heaven!

It's the perfect occasion to crack the champagne, and so Chance obliges with a bottle of the finest Napa. We drink, we laugh, and we make love with utter abandon. The night is ours until we decide otherwise. As a reminder, the cathedral's bell rings the hour. I don't remember it doing so when I lived in Monterey, but if it does now, it is meant to be. Like all things of perfect timing, of synchronicity, when life leads to the beat of its own drum, it's always meant to be. We make love until we fall off the last embrace.

— o —

I am slightly hangovered, but complete. I smell of sex, but I am in no rush to wipe the night clean. Chance is still sleeping the sleep of the just; he is an angel amid a broken sea of crumpled sheets and covers. I am wearing his t-shirt, which is like three sizes too big, venturing on the deck to surrender to the ocean breeze. How blessed we are to live in this world, this beautiful world of ours. Now couldn't be a better time to renew my allegiance to protecting it. The ills I have been feeling in my bones since building the Bayville *bridge* will be met with the might of the watchful keeper. It is my solemn promise to the Program and the denizens of my world. Someone's got to feel the passion!

— o —

After an improvised but copious breakfast, Chance and I ready ourselves to test our progress. We cross over to the sleazy motel in *San Francisco* wherefrom we hop to my house in Bayville. After a quick break to double-check on our position, we make it to the other motel—the nice one—then hit north again to the *Bayville* house where I introduce Chance to Little Honda. Before you know it, we're back at the Monterey beach

135

cottage! Including some unpredicted time-shifting, we are done in less than two hours. Note to self: *time shifts*.

So, that's how the Governor does it; he has a map, he has clear pictures, and he goes wherever he wishes. Except, I suspect his map is huge, since he has done it for a long, *long* time.

Because it is consuming and rather illogical to travel all the way to Buenos Aires to locate a suitable landing spot into *A's*, we decide to do research from my house in *Bayville*. Chance is mesmerized by the fact I live with a foot in both camps. Now I can share the fun!

I don't know how the Governor was able to straighten the paperwork for my stay on *A's side*, but I sense we're going to require his help for Chance—he too needs to get covered. It's easy, because the Governor shows up in the office just when we have our backs turned to the chair. He must like that chair!

He welcomes Chance to the team (the team?), congratulating him on his keen vision. The Governor doesn't mean to not include me; he makes sure that I get my share of the credits. He's here to help the Prof with his spy kit. It couldn't be a more perfect time to ask how he comes up with paperwork as if out of a hat. *Simple*, he says, *just like building bridges, you have to set your mind to it.* And how, may I ask? *When I don't have to show up, you'll have your answer!* As usual, all is said, nothing is said; that's the Governor! And as usual, he's gone before anyone has a chance to say goodbye. I swear, one of these days, I'm going to follow him!

——— o ———

136

20 – INVESTIGATION

Bayville (both) are our new headquarters. We have a huge map of Buenos Aires, as well as one of the Argentines pinned to the office walls.

I almost forgot: before he left, the Governor announced that Chance had joined the ranks of *designers*. Of course, the Prof is delighted!

But before we get too involved with South Continent, there is a party in San Francisco to which we must attend. As it so conveniently turns out, it is in honour of John's return to his teaching job in B.A., and it is expected his wife will be there too. I promise that by the end of that event I will know her name, but I can't promise it will be as good as *the wife*!

Once more, we book a room in each of the motels, just in case we need to cross. This time, there won't be any hydromobiles or Little Hondas to take us there; it will be just a leap from the office to San Francisco. Though, I don't want to make a habit of it, because I love my rides!

On another note, it goes without saying that I have been keeping on feeding *A* my story as it develops. Our connection is secure, and I love the man more every day. Chance will never replace him and vice versa—just in case you needed to know.

— o —

The party is at the other end of town, by the piers. Ships destined for the Asian and South Continental cities are awaiting their turn to be unmoored. I think of Rio,

Adelaide, and Le Havre—not that the boat for Le Havre docks here—but I think about the French city anyway. I *think* of my travels in breaths of emotions, as recurring déja vus of alien passions. It is how I feel as the sun sets beyond the Golden Gate.

— o —

The event plays in one of the lofts of a red brick building near Jackson Square. It is a large space—the size of a gallery—that tastefully highlights the recent work by the resident artiste, one of the Program's best-known painters.

We arrive early enough to not bump into groups as we tour the exhibit, but it doesn't take long before the place becomes alive with the loud, undulating jumble of words and laughter.

We walk the floor, beckoned by past acquaintances, while keeping an eye on the entrance for the arrival of our suspects. I don't have to go over the mundane details of what is said, just that it is the predictable stuff of conversation, neither boring nor captivating. The idea here is to enjoy the human company. Chance is having a field day with his students present and past, while I rekindle friendships with the few from my time in Monterey. I recognize surprise faces from Straßburg and Adelaide; we wave at each other with big smiles and bright eyes. For some reason, Chantal comes to haunt my thoughts; she hasn't been in there for a long time, not since the crossing to Rio with Chance. *How is she doing?* I wonder.

Finally the grand entrance! *The wife* is locking arms with John; she is taller than him by at least ten centimetres due to the fact she wears stilettos. My female instincts immediately home on her domineering persona. She needs to be the center of attention, with the pointed arrogance of those who could care less about what others think of them. She is above criticism and idolatry; she stamps the wood floor with the official seal of the *fuck-you-all* department. *The chill* is on.

Chance rejoins me, conveying in no uncertain terms that he is feeling what I feel. The mood has turned a shade darker, while no-one else notices. The crowd goes through the motions, played at the hands of a greater, overseeing actor—a puppeteer with no love for her puppets. I know it is still an experiment, just like in the last party, but the group is substantially larger and *the chill* ever more powerful. I wonder why the guests are incapable of noticing the change. I intuit it could be because the effect is of alien nature, as if all the negativity of *A's world* had been distilled into an essence, which *the wife* wears as a perfume. But Chance and I are immune to the hypnosis, although we are concerned about being noticed because of it—it calls for a guise. We modify our shields to accommodate the necessary overlay; something we can thank our advanced training for!

The timing seems so perfect when John waves at us that, for an instant, I believe we're being set up. The couple proceeds towards us, greeting acquaintances on the way. *The wife* walks as if she were modeling for one of the big fashion designers, rolling her hips in a cascade of liquid moves. Finally, we greet each other. I presume that from the distance, we look like old friends. It is said that space marries assumptions in the oddest of ways, but who's to know? What I mean is that the four of us put up a good front. John introduces *the wife* as Consuelo, an apt name for irony in her case: Consuelo, *Queen of Ice and Unease*. I am sticking to *the wife*! She looks at us with mocking in her eyes. *I will crush you*, they say. *Fuck you, Consuelo! You want dark, I give you dark!* But I step back; no need to sound the bugle of our presence—I feel the bitch all the same. Chance is more stoic about it, putting on charm to draw her into confidence. *It won't work, Chance!* OK, I'm losing it again—I settle once and for all. My job is to investigate without looking like a fumbling detective. All my antennas are out when I chat with John. I need a solid readout on where he's at. Is he *villain* or is he *toy*? I don't come near anything that indicates he wants to harm the Program, but I definitely get that he is dangerous to it. In this case he is *toy*, a toy belonging to Ms. Consuelo, agent from the dark world of *A*. But Chance is working her, and he might, against her will, extract something that she doesn't want to give. Perhaps she should have thought about taking it easy on the perfume.

A second ago, I thought Chance wouldn't have, well, a chance; but I have now reconsidered. The man is likely more resourceful than I have been willing to admit. Perhaps sleeping with him has bred familiarity and an element of un-bestowing on my part. But I'm still speaking with John who's starting to notice my absentmindedness. Instead of losing interest, he exclaims, *Consuelo, can you believe that we're in the presence of two first-generation teachers: Six and Seven!?* She looks at us with a slight tilt of the head, mildly curious, but also amused. I sense she is made pleased by the nuance. We may serve her as a matched pair with valuable consecutive numbers. But she doesn't realize that her mannerism is giving her away. There is a good reason for it: she is unaware of being guilty before proven so. Chance and I are fond of reversed investigating; we know she's bad, possibly an ill-minded intruder from *A's world*, so why try confirming the obvious when we need to probe for reasons? But my mental process is working counter to what is being played between us, for there is congeniality, enough of it to allow for plans to form. We are invited to join them in Buenos Aires, when the Professor and I visit the Chapter next month. *Good work, Chance, you're the man!* We part with polite hugs, feigning imperviousness to *the chill*, but I notice things are somewhat bouncier in the room. *The wife* even manages the start of a natural smile. She and John casually move on to the next group.

While scanning the place for the last time before leaving, my attention is caught by a face ringing of the familiar in a kind of lost way. It takes me the longest time to put a name to it: Corbyn, the odd student from Adelaide, who is said to have turned the Chapter to the authorities for wrongdoing. I always doubted it; he was a fine young man—just different. He hasn't seen me and I don't wish to connect. Time to go! Chance and I have got a lot of extrapolating awaiting us at the office.

— o —

Before returning to Bayville, we spent two days at the San Francisco motel by the beach, loosely going over notes, but mostly, enjoying each other.

The office is now in full hopping mode between the two worlds, as we are getting familiarized with Buenos Aires and the Argentines at large. We deem the office of my original house to be the one safe space where we keep most of our important information away from

141

potential scrutiny. Neither of us trusts *Bayville* or its people, especially its police and the various branches of government of its state and country. The unnecessary violence, breaches of privacy, and the countless critical errors committed by these agencies are emblematic of the fundamental corruption of *A's world*. It is the social version of bad air, excessive noise, and the assault on the environment. I am aware that a vast swath of its denizens consider the place livable at a high level of standards, but these souls are oblivious to the cost. I would go as far as saying that awareness is near zero at the gregarious level, not to mention their mind and body connection at the personal end. To contemplate good living amid a global catastrophe says it all! Although it may make sense in the context of individual selfishness; humans are indubitably a social species whose downfall is foreseen in the deconstruction of its collective makeup. There is no way around it. It doesn't mean that I consider lone wolves the problem—we have those here as well, to no consequence. I am talking about individual greed, which is nothing but another word for the stigma of social greed. That being said, my house in Bayville is safer by far.

While going over the logistics of the investigation, we have ample time to rummage through the fine details of what *bridge-building* truly entices, and its connection with the origins of the Program. It's obvious that neither of us are pioneers in *bridge* design, for I suspect its principles have been there all along. When you understand that there is an entirely functional world across a threshold reached by an inner connection, such as one with a *character* of *tale-making*—A, say—you start imagining safe-enough places to reach across. I realize that the act of disappearing and reappearing out of thin air belongs to the predictable and unverifiable fancy of deep fiction, of which you might consider my explanations to be nothing but the figment of my *character's* imagination; there is nothing I can do to assure you that it isn't. You are just going to have to be brave and bear with me. So, when you create thereof a strong enough image of a point of arrival from a recallable point of departure, you are good to go. Of course, that can only happen when one has been trained to believe in such things, and not without the assistance of the collective force that is the Program. In other words, no-one outside Chance and Janette's world should be capable of such an act. I know, I know— I give then take back; I am incorrigible that way. Feel free to chastise me!

We hypothesize that the Governor uses portals that could have been around since humans first appeared on the planet. I am saying that because we believe there are two sorts of *bridges*: those, like ours, that self-erase after use; and the ones that are fixed, which based on our speculations, are the kinds utilized by lovely Consuelo, and potentially, other agents from *A's side*. The point is how do we find them? This also brings to our attention the plausibility that we could still own the patent on *erasables*, and that before me and Chance, no such means of travel existed. And that is why the Governor put us in charge! He, to this point, was the only one aware of the possibility, whether he was able to create his own or not. By extension, he must have been using *fixed bridges* all along, to which the chair in my office belongs. Just a hypothesis, but Chance is all for investigating that angle and finding the trigger. So, another day, another item on the list—I might as well rejoice at the thought it will never end!

Of course, for now, we must concentrate on how to reach Buenos Aires without the use of the intercontinental soft-rail system, or the express ship line. Did I say we don't have airplanes? It was not something that appealed to us, as we witnessed the carnage of first attempts. Of course, we have the small one-person unit for the enthusiast, but it is limited to specific recreational air space. But back to Buenos Aires!

At any rate, we don't have much time left to prepare for the Argentines. John and *the wife* are under the assumption that we already are on our way by now. Time flies when you're having fun! But in all seriousness, we have to create a *bridge* to there without landing into an embarrassing situation, or worse. But staying on our side, as already mentioned, is a lot less dangerous than crossing over without a good plan. We have what we need to take care of that when we make it down there.

---- o ----

21 – BUENOS AIRES

We reach Buenos Aires directly from the office. We lucked out; our landing pad is the studio of one of the Rio students presently on travels to the Osaka Chapter, and who so generously offered for us to stay there during his absence. The keys are with the concierge, but it makes no difference to us—we didn't need them to get in—we will collect them on the way down instead.

The aerial view of the Japanese Gardens and the surrounding parks from the top-story windows is to die for. B.A. is a lot like San Francisco, gorgeous and made for species co-habitation. It is what Rio should be like, but since we've been hearing good things about Rio lately, we have hopes that one day the city will compete with the best.

John and *the wife* live near the *Rio Dique* yacht club, a manageable walk to and from the University of Buenos Aires where the Chapter is located.

The soirée is not scheduled until two days from now, but since we must play the part, we shall stop by the school as promised. We don't need a reason for it; all senior members are welcome to appear as they wish.

We meet John before his class to say hello. He introduces us to his students who are delighted by our presence. A visit from First-Generation professors is a rare treat received with the customary ovation. In the eyes of new students, we are heroes, especially in view of accomplishments that have lifted the Program to a level rivaled by no other institution. It goes without saying that my work in *tale-making* is creating quite a stir, to the point at which John begs me to teach a class tomorrow. I oblige. We also learn that *the wife* is out on business and will not return until we get together for dinner. I had hoped to connect before the date, but it surprises neither of us—*business* meaning that she is most likely kept busy with dubious affairs.

Chance and I immediately take off for the site of our planned *bridge* into *A's world*. If successful, we will be able to access both of its sides from any point. In the midst of our research at the *Bayville* office, we zeroed in on an ideal location common to the two realities: *Cementerio de la Recoleta*, in a recessed spot between a pair of mausoleums shaded by trees. Problem is, the cemetery is quite busy and closes at 5:30. We take it that our miraculous appearance will suit the spirit of the place; but most plausibly, as in my observation of the Governor's ins and outs, it will happen when everyone's back is turned. It seems that the private nature of a *bridge*, and hopefully, a *self-erasable* one as well, extends to the act of leaving and arriving. Once again, it proves true!

Cementerio de la Recoleta is a place where time is still attached to the past. Just like every other city in *A's world*, *Buenos Aires* is riding on organized chaos. But inside the cemetery, all the noise becomes muffled as if not allowed to breach the sanctity of the space and disturb the quietude of those meeting with loved ones. Save for the pesky tourists, it is a place of deep connection between the living and the dead. It is my hope that our brief presence is of no consequence to these reunions.

But my thoughts get jolted out of their clouds by a different kind of visitor. I am absolutely certain she is not here to remember the dead. As a matter of fact she isn't expected here anymore than *the wife* was expected at the taqueria in *San Francisco*. I remember her name: McKenzie Henderson, head investigator in the Adelaide Chapter case. So, the abject woman is showing her true colours—she is one of them! Of course, *them* meaning her and *the wife* for the time. I make sure to turn around as she passes, a reflex which may serve our investigation, but does a great disservice to my desire to confront her for what she did then, which I took as a nasty manœuvre to undo the Chapter. It all makes sense now, and for that, I bestow upon her the rightful title of *the bitch*!

— o —

As Chance and I are being let in, we're told that we are expected to join a party with friends of Consuelo's at a popular club afterwards. Of course, we accept and look forward to meeting with new faces. With a glance, Chance communicates that it might be a trap, but then again, any error on our parts could easily turn the tables around. I silently suggest we treat the invitation as a gift to enjoy. If all plays as envisioned, we don't expect to be met with *a chill* at a gathering organized by *the wife*—one way to know whether she deserves the guilty verdict or not! Then again, in this business, we are so constantly misled by false positives and negatives, that it is better to let the currents carry us.

— o —

The dinner is a small affair, but surprisingly delicious. We didn't expect *the wife* to be quite the talented chef, but she excels at it, and so does John. We are not meeting any of the weirdness of the previous

147

encounters, to the point of me feeling that Chance and I imagined the whole thing. We also prepared for open word-sparring between us, but it never comes to that. Frankly, I am both disappointed and relieved by the civility that prevails. *The wife*, if I may still call her by that name, is a delightful hostess capable of witty humor. At this very moment, I quite like her, which makes it hard for me to justify the picture I drew of her. That being said, part of me isn't buying my sudden reversal. It goes: *Don't be fooled, Janette; you know what she's up to!*

I tend to trust the messenger in my head over the trickery of self-doubt, so, instead of relaxing my mind, I put it on guard duty. Too much unexplained sweetness is bound to conceal the sour and bitter of deceit. I sense Chance is not buying it either. It smells of a setup.

— o —

The four of us walk the distance from the apartment to the club. It's a beautiful night glittering with a mix of soft-glow lights and stars; so much more soothing than the assault of neons and fluorescents on the other side. We barely hear the drone of traffic from the foliaged pedestrian trails that crisscross the city. I could love this place. It only takes a half hour to reach the gates of the club—I feel rejuvenated.

It's a private party that forgoes the usual wildness of the premises. Apparently, Consuelo and her *firm* rented the space for the occasion, mainly a gathering of fashion designers, high-end cosmetics formulation chemists, and models. The interesting thing is that the field is fairly new and caters to a counter-cultural element. The Program has recently looked into it in order to define its dynamics.

Neither Chance nor I know what came of it, but considering the circumstances, the results are bound to reach us before long. The whole idea feels imported, but wherefrom is the question. Vogue is vogue, but placement to coax is another animal altogether. It is what I smell as we step inside the club.

Sure enough, the whole thing rings of fakeness. Needless to say that to these people, it is a statement meant to represent the latest trending thing. *The wife* has left us for her people, so I ask John when, exactly, the fashion was introduced. According to him, it just kind of popped up everywhere at once not too long ago—*A neo-vogue in reflection of the times*, he says. Whoa, am I getting old or what!? John wishes us a good time, excusing himself to rejoin his partner. I guess we're here to make some friends!

I don't normally drink but since the drug of choice is alcohol, I am having wine. I forget that other countries are still into inebriants; but then, I haven't much time to reflect on the nuance when *the bitch* from Adelaide brushes by me. I don't have to ask myself what the fuck she's doing here; we know where she's from and the cemetery where she crossed; but for Christ's sake, I didn't touch the wine and my head's already spinning!

I nudge Chance. *Good grief, man, this is a meeting of agents from the other side!* He gets it. We don't know whether we've been uncovered or not, or if danger is looming. We have a good chance to remain incognito by keeping on emitting the Program's aura; any sign of having been in *A's world* will give us away. That is the test *the wife* has been reserving for us; she suspects we have been on her tail. Now I really feel like getting drunk; something I haven't done since Straßburg.

Before I have my first sip, Consuelo is on us, enquiring about how we are enjoying the party. *Fine, just fine!* we say. I excuse myself; purposely leaving Chance with her while I look for the bathrooms. May he handle her; he knows what to do! I finally drink my wine in one straight take. It hits me squarely—I already feel better!

— o —

As much as I would love for Chance to be part of the narrative, he's not the one reporting to *A*. If you must know, he talks as much as I do. I would say that we are on a par as a team. Whatever he has in seniority over me, I have in Program innovation; it's a good balance.

It's ironic to find ourselves guests of an assembly bent on flirting with Program members for no other purpose than positioning themselves on a game board of their own making. Tonight we are shown a breadth of perspective hardly imagined. They are organized, corrupt, and intent on detrimentally influencing our world, while ruining our healing efforts in theirs. There is little doubt they will go after *A* if they know he is my *character*.

For the sake of clarity, their group includes men as well—not just *wives* and *bitches*! Moreover, I am under the conviction that they aren't limited to this gathering. For now, we stand amid them, uncertain of what's ahead.

As I return, Chance is still in deep conversation with *the wife*, except this time, *the bitch* has joined in. I pretend to not know her, but it is she, instead, who prompts the obligatory, *Have we met before?* I look at her straight in the eyes, *Adelaide? What brings you here?* She is now a representative of *the Firm*'s Terra Australisian branch, on business in Buenos Aires. *And how is business*

150

doing? I ask. *Better every day!* I wonder what she refers to, the Program, or Chance and I in particular? I sense the up-notching of the game, the winding of the coil; no doubt now that we were brought in to be exposed. We're the reason for the party!

Where do we stand, dumb Program folks or spies? Presently, it's a tie. As the act unravels, more of the de jure guests seek our attention. One by one they probe with innocent questions, innuendos, jest, and implicity. They each return to the hive to add to the honeycomb, out of which a final verdict will be drawn. It doesn't matter whether we leave or stay, so we decide to stay and see if there's something we can turn to our advantage. It's mere wishful thinking, but then again, in spite of the appearances, they don't necessarily have the upper hand. Unless we have been spotted in *A's world*—which would mean that we have been outplayed—they're most likely testing us against the farce that is *the Firm*, hence Chance's question as *the wife* and *the bitch* return: *Are you sure this new trend is what our young have been anxious to evolve into? It feels rather alien!* Well, as I observe, the little eye twinkles die one by one—it's our turn to bring on *the chill*. Not what they expected, apparently. We are just a pair of obtuse Program *designers* of little use—neither friend nor foe. It's not a game-changer, but we are now assured that Consuelo and her peers have no idea what we're up to. The lesson calls for upping vigilance if we must get to the bottom of what it is they are brewing. Though, as per this present, it's obvious the Program is the target and that it's time to think about protecting it.

In a sudden turn around, the party loses its steam as we see agents leave. We're no longer of interest to them. Finally, John rejoins us to socialize.

We politely edge our way out by thanking *the wife* and a few of the more insistent diggers and instigators. *What a lovely party, sorry it ended so quickly!* Chance can't help himself when sarcasm walks right in—my kind of man! I swear *the bitch* could kill us with her looks if she wasn't smiling. We're finally outside, thanking John and wishing him good luck with his teaching. *The wife* is gone. We are ready for the long walk to the studio that overlooks the Japanese Garden. Chance and I kiss.

———— o ————

22 – EARLY YEARS WITHOUT A

We are in the month of October 2000, fourteen years since Buenos Aires. The main reason for the jump is that I lost *A* right after returning to Bayville from the Argentines, the result of which brought me great distress. There was nothing Chance could do to alleviate my sense of imbalance. I feared *A* had died with my story.

My parents have now moved in with me and Chance is back in Monterey. But you should know that the investigation is still going strong. Yes, it's a bitch of a case, if you may excuse the language! If you are guessing that *A* and I have been reunited, you guess right; it happened on the 2nd of July, roughly three months ago. I shall spare you the details, but know that he is fine, and that my story is back on track. I never saw John again until a month ago when we bumped into each other at a downtown gallery. He was a changed man, still in the Program, but somewhat diminished by what *the wife* had put him through. I shall get to it in due time.

So what happened after the party in Buenos Aires? It's a long story, but since *A* is now back at his old post, it is naturally my main objective to tell it.

— o —

We returned to Bayville to put our notes and observations in order. We needed to come up with the means to protect the Program—a plan. It struck us that McKenzie Henderson, aka *the bitch*, had likely used a fixed platform to cross worlds, and so we earmarked the item as one of extreme importance—we had to find those *bridges* and map the entire network. Of course, we didn't think it would simply happen in a moment of brilliance.

Chance had suggested investigating the chair used by the Governor on his visits to the house. The idea was great, but how to go about it? Unlike *erasables*, which required specific *destination images* proprietary to the traveler; with *fixed bridges*, you had to work from a map. We knew the chair was one of two sympathetic office points, but it was also a hub from which other places could be reached. The Governor's den was my first option, a guess as good as any other. I sat in the chair, holding Chance's hand. I closed my eyes, visualizing the Gov's office as I last remembered it. Sure enough, I found myself in Straßburg, across the desk from which I first heard about the Program. I was alone; Chance didn't make it and the Governor was nowhere in sight. It was an impressive first try, which left me pretty satisfied with myself. Just as I began worrying about Chance's whereabouts, he materialized right behind me; apparently, *the bridge* only took one passenger at a time—no *erasable* there! Now, that we had made it to a *fixed point* inside our world, we were eager to find others. We returned to Bayville. The only way to prove whether the Buenos Aires cemetery concealed a *fixed bridge* or not, was to be brave and give it a try. This time, Chance went first. I waited exactly one minute before following. The Prof was there, standing barely fifty yards away from our place of arrival a few days prior. We had found where *the bitch* had crossed!

But we were still in our world. Now, we wanted to see how *that bridge* would take us to *A's side*. In an instant, we reached the other end, at *Cementerio de la*

Recoleta, in roughly the same spot. It was enough for a day—we quickly made our way back to the office. It was obvious that both *fixed* and *erasable systems* functioned on similar principals, and could work together side by side: one required memorized prints from a map, whereas the other offered the versatility of any chosen point, as long as the image was strong enough. I also had a hunch that the two systems could be linked. As it turned out, I was right. It also turned out that I was indeed the inventor of the *erasable*, the one achievement that has kept us ahead of *the Firm* to this point. Now, you get it: *the Firm* is the Program's dark foe from *A's world*. But before we go there, let's return to our case circa 1986.

— o —

Now that we had established that there existed a réseau of *fixed bridges*, we committed to intensifying our research into, mainly: who designed them, when, and how much of it had been accessed by *the Firm*. Since we knew our chair could take us to various points, my idea was to pick one of the oldest structures on Earth and see if we could link. Chance came up with the Megalithic Temples of Malta. You could always count on him for an unusual suggestion, but it was a good one, because we were there in an instant. Yes, that proved it; these *bridges* went as far back as 3,000 BC. In his excitement, Chance wanted to try all of the oldest archeological sites, but I reminded him that *the Firm* probably didn't care about rock structures, unless of course, they made ideal places for fashion and cosmetics shows. What I always loved about Chance was his hearty laughter, and how readily he was triggered by my poor sense of humour. To me, it was the kind of spirited response that made the human proximity so endearing. It was particularly critical at the time I lost *A*.

Nothing is ever a sure thing when dealing with the unknown; yet, when is anything truly a sure thing?!

At the time, we mostly relied on faith to keep on. Anyone could have built a *bridge* on any old site and call it ancient, but we chose to embrace anything novel with abandon over doubt. We probably learned more from intuition than from such soft facts as dating *bridges* based on location. Trust was of the essence, and it kept on propelling us forward. In a moment of silliness, we left a message on the Governor's desk: *Sorry to have missed you!* The next morning, one word: *Congratulations!* was stuck to the office chair. It meant we were on the right track. Of course, no solid help!

One thing led to another, and before long we had mapped over one hundred *fixed points*, each with a correspondency in *A*'s reality. It soon became obvious that *fixed bridges* stopped being built around the turn of the twentieth century when the two worlds were truly coming apart. We believed that originally, those *bridges* were meant to connect with each other, but the design could not accommodate the widening distance between the two realities; and so, *the science* became a lost art, so to speak. Along that line of speculation, we also started to believe that the Program was responsible for its creation, which naturally sent us reeling into all kinds of scenarios concerning the Governor. He had said that *bridge-building* would eventually shed light on his whatabouts; we thus trusted that we were homing in on him. As far as projection went, it was easy for Chance and I to envisage the Governor as a form of energy capable of shape-shifting. For now, he was a very tall man, but who—or what—was he during the Neolithic Period of the Malta temples? Perhaps Chance was spot on about wanting to visit all the old archeological digs. Was it possible that the original system was meant to connect all the sacred sites to each other; each a part vital to the makeup of a grand monument shrouding the planet? Our heads exploded, but it didn't cool off the excitement—we were on a roll. And then the Program, the Chapters, each a temple in its own right; the new *self-erase bridges* that were built across the two branches of the split reality, all oddly forming pictures of an alliance between the old and the new; and for what reason: to build an ultimate bridge across time? The thought hurt all portions of my brain; Chance sighed, resolute to the inevitability of losing his sanity. But we knew how to step back and let love cut through the thick— success was measured by the whorl of a wild embrace.

— o —

With all of the action, it didn't mean that I never crossed into *Bayville* to take Little Honda on rides; we went out, if just for the sake of the romance between us. Actually, she is still with me to this day, just as pretty as the first time we met; still parked in the comfy corner of the garage that I arranged for her. Chance jokingly called me a fetishist at the time, but I'm just a sentimentalist that sees a living force in everything. I have no doubt she will live forever, at least in my thoughts.

Actually, as part of the investigation, we frequently forayed into *A's world* to monitor *the Firm's* traffic, map their meeting points, and identify their habits. By then, our expert use of *erasables*, practically allowed us to go anywhere from any place with nary a glitch. The miracle of

157

my invention was that if a crossing wasn't meant to be—meaning dangerous—it didn't allow for it. So, there was no such thing as being timid or reckless in that regard. The items to never slack on were stealth and vigilance. Once suspected of spying on *the Firm*, one was forever on their radar. Though it wasn't necessarily a good thing that we were no longer invited to their fashion shows.

Since we're on the subject of *Firm* meetings, Chance and I came across Corbyn—the odd Adelaide student—at one such gathering in Osaka; his partner was no other than McKenzie Henderson, or *the bitch*. That was a case of *full circle* that pointed vividly in the direction of agents having corrupted students one on one. As it turned out, all of the known *Firm* members, males and females, were either married or in close relationships with students, professors, or other working members of the Program, including *tale-makers*. At that point, there was no other option but to strategize.

— o —

The time couldn't have been riper to enter the defense stage. The Governor, taking advantage of Chance's acumen, offered him the position of *head designer* of Program protection. I was to remain in charge of *bridge-building* and continue with my leading role in *tale-making*; though I have to admit that I had neglected that end because of *A's* absence, reversing to intense soul-searching instead.

Chance and I resumed with working as a team on the investigation, melding our redefined assignments into a force of greater wingspan. The Prof recruited students specifically suited for his new course in Program defense,

158

and taught—courtesy *the erasables*—at all Chapters. Chance's aim was to turn the group into specialists capable of monitoring *Firm* corruption, tallying casualties, and barring students and faculty from the proximity of existing vulnerabilities. It was a formidable task in the face of sheer numbers, and even more so considering *the Firm* couldn't suspect it was under heavy surveillance. What Chance wasn't able to take care of I made my responsibility, notably *tale-makers*, the most troublesome part of the investigation. Their relationships with *characters* were private and immune to scrutiny. We had no means of probing their minds to know who was on the other end, and what story was being told. Their role was to encrypt messages to the best of their unique skills, ideally the ones in line with their education and training. But nothing could prevent some of them from corrupting the data and turning *A's world* into a worse Hell.

— o —

After a year of consolidating our position against *the Firm*, we refocused our attention to the system of *fixed bridges* and its history. As we had speculated, the Governor was one of the early *designers* of a system of communication that tied all of the *sacred sites*; sacred only in the way of interpretation across the ages—there was nothing sacred about them; it was simply science. The Governor was—and still is—a mystery unwilling to answer the basic question of his origins; all he kept on saying was, *Let's save the best part for last!* But he didn't mind talking about the *bridges* now that we had pretty much exposed a hefty number of them. The temples were centers that played a part in the mapping of the cosmos.

When connected, either in groups or as a whole, they became one, with the specific role of monitoring a portion of the heavens, or the entire galactic complex. Modern science had no part in it, while the ancient knowledge at the base of the making of physical reality had all to do with it.

As this story is not about recalling the beginning steps of humanity, I shall forego the details in favour of focusing on what pertains to the case. The *bridges* linking the temples were a unique, fixed network meant to carry energy between power centers; they could also be used as gateways for engineers. A secondary réseau was built throughout time until the split of 1870. While there were other such splits through the ages, the system was only partially affected. But because of advances in technology and the advent of exploratory social mechanics, the last of them was fatal to the science of *bridge-building*—as neither in my world nor in *A*'s was the original design any longer applicable. My *self-erasable* version is the official replacement to the *fixed network*. To my pride and joy, the future of the Program became dependent on two of my achievements: *bridge-building* and *tale-making*.

In 1900, the Program shut the old system down. The last of the *fixed bridges* was built in 1899, in my house, two years after it was erected. It was the Governor's residence, and one of the few buildings that rose in both realities after the split. The Gov made sure of it since he owned both places!

— o —

And so, it is how my office chair became an access point to the entire *original network*, and also how I was made the owner of the second house—by the Governor transferring the title to my name. But that isn't answering to how said *system* became available to *the Firm*.

— o —

Contrarily to what one might think, *the Firm* doesn't go back as far as the temples. In fact, it only started using the *bridges* when the Governor reopened the *network*, a decade or so before reinstating the Program.

Chance and I speculated that a grudge could have been what started it all—something to do with the budding petrochemical industry of the 19th century. We had been looking into who was responsible for the US joining France against Prussia, only to come against a wall, as if it just had happened for no explainable reason. It was how we arrived at hypothesizing that the Governor had something to do with it, and that someone who was to lose a fortune because of it, found out. We stipulated that John D. Rockefeller, seeing his dream turn to smoke after the US and French defeat, and the parceling of the United States into three countries, began to draw the plan for his revenge. From there, it was only a matter of time before he discovered the *bridge system* and started mapping it; until, of course, the Governor shut it down in 1900. But we only found traces of the man in our reality up to that point, and then he vanished. That effectively ruined our theory and complicated our research exponentially, until we contemplated the possibility that after crossing, he got stuck in *A's world*. That, of course, created a paradox, since he already existed in that reality, making a fortune in oil. In fact, the *bridge network* was the paradox; hence why it was shut down—one couldn't be two—that was the bottom line. In the event one implausibly crossed after system closure, it wasn't hard to imagine that he or she would find themselves in a state of suspension until the reactivation of the *bridges*, which we postulated could have been the case with Rockefeller, and a good reason for him to retaliate against the Governor and the Program. It all made sense in theory, except that John D. might have had nothing to do with it.

So, for the purpose of the story, and in respect to my rule of keeping names out of it, let's just say that the man in question was simply known as *the CEO—the CEO of the Firm.*

Chance and I stuck to that version and never turned back. We established that *the Firm* was founded in late 1961 with a team of agents recruited from *A*'s side, for the purpose of finding the Governor and destroying his work, which *the CEO* defined as everything that had evolved on our side since 1870, as well as anything aimed at saving *A's world* in the process—in other words: the Program. *The Firm* had a lot of catching up to do, namely, making boatloads of money in record time. *The CEO* was a specialist at making fortunes, and before long, he was buying his way into both the cosmetics and entertainment industries, owning clubs and larger venues on both sides, and wedging his way into corrupting the young here, with bogus fashions. His enormous income was for the sole purpose of building his team into a force that would ultimately do the Program in, consequently erasing our reality. That was the theory in a nutshell!

Pretty much all of our work was based on intuition and the nerve to stick with it, right or wrong. And you know, somehow we made steady progress, eventually encircling the whole *Firm network* without them knowing. We had tallied their numbers, anticipated their movements and gatherings, but ironically, we had no idea how to defeat them. The reason was simple: ethically, we couldn't just start an outright war; that impulse strictly belonged to *A's world* where hitmen could have been hired to do the dirty work. We had an advantage, yet we couldn't capitalize on it.

Chance suggested that we shut the *fixed bridges*; an idea that had floated at my end, but that I hadn't shared yet. It was a good option, since we could have locked them into *A*'s reality without a means for them to ever cross onto our side again. But nothing was that simple. *The Firm* existed equally on both sides, well aware the *system* could be closed without notice. *The CEO* was confident the *fixed bridges* were there to stay, counting on the Governor's dependence on the *network* for his travels. Amusingly, *the Firm* was oblivious to the fact *erasables* were close to becoming his new means of getting around.

I hope you're still with me.

— o —

It wasn't all work, mind you. Chance and I enjoyed life regardless of which side we were on. Some of the research was downright recreational, and we didn't feel particularly guilty relishing those opportunities. We often visited with our friends in Monterey during those moments when the mind was overworked and the flesh left starving for sexual exploration. Alice and Max were always down for some legitimate fun the old-fashioned way, and they never disappointed. It always was the best of times when us four shared life together.

There was also *Three* with whom I had co-taught in Adelaide, who was always up for guests in her lively home. Save for the times of my breakdowns, she and I had stayed in touch throughout the years, sharing the joys and the pains with equal abandon. She no longer was teaching, but had opted to remain in Terra Australis to pursue her heartfelt calling for the realms of *tale-making*. She was one of our bests, I believed. With *bridges* at our disposal, it was easy for Chance and I to visit; so we made it as often as we could. Not so for *Three* when she came our way—*bridge-building* was still off-limit—but she made the trip once a year nonetheless. There was something special about First-Generation professors getting together, a mystique that went extremely deep in the form of silent, ancient knowing. We became one, just like the temples did when connected; very much a gestaltic whole larger than the sum of *Three*, *Six* and *Seven*, if I may be allowed the jest.

— o —

Chance and his crew had isolated the corrupt *tale-makers*, but just like with *the Firm*, we were in no position to do anything, because we didn't truly understand the nature of the corruption. We had hypothesized that the damage was in the form of undoing what some of our other *story-tellers* had started; but its fundamentals remained a complete mystery at our end. We suspected that some freak element was at play, that perhaps those *tale-makers* had been set in reversed polarity by *the Firm*. By that, I mean, instead of sending the good word to *A's world*, they carried bad seeds from it, idea figments meant to infiltrate the social fiber, as in the case of the tasteless fashion trends hitting all corners of the planet. Essentially, we were left in the dark as far as the impact on the program was concerned. We treated the case as a matter of dire circumstances without the ability to gauge the extent of what *the Firm* could inflict on our universe. Once I wondered if it wasn't simply a hoax; another of those *untaught* lessons by the Governor. But it was a far-fetched presumption.

The dilemma lay in how to extract the corruption. In any other world, it would have been a simple matter of purging the bad blood out of the Program, by sending the bankrupt elements reeling into irremediable madness, as it was suspected would happen when one was erased. But we didn't have the heart for it. It was the great cost of caring for all things living, the dark within virtue. But what of the agents if we did? Surely *the CEO* didn't just count on student and faculty to self-destruct—too many of us were untouched. We feared that the removal of suspects would end up being nothing but trouble in the light of their intimate associations with operatives of *the Firm*. We had a lot of work to do if we planned to keep on wearing silk gloves; and perhaps, not enough time for it.

There was a grave concern that had lingered for the longest time regarding the *fixed bridges* and the vulnerability of my own office. Should my place become known to *the Firm*, all of what we did would have been for nothing. Of course, the same applied to the Governor.

It just happened that on one of his routine visit to *Bayville*, Chance almost ran into *the wife*. We knew she had no business being there, certainly nothing related to fashion—not *Bayville*'s forte. The situation left us to ponder on whether we were back on *the Firm's* big radar or if it was just a fluke. But please! No, she was there to look for something specific—and even perhaps the Governor's old residence!

Chance didn't just hide and scamper; he followed her. She nonchalantly walked the streets, taking pictures with a small rangefinder camera, but never came close to the house. Within a block of the theatre, she turned into an alley and was gone.

We hadn't yet found another *fixed bridge* in town. *The wife* made it obvious others existed that needed uncovering. It was a disturbing revelation that shattered the relative safety of the office in our own Bayville.

From that point on, it became necessary to apply vigilance on both sides with equal importance. We already knew we couldn't just leave the house in *A's world* abandoned; that would have invited continuous break-ins, vandalism, and squatting. But the proximity of other *bridges* forced us to take turns in making ourselves even more visible. We did yard work, shopped at the neighbourhood stores, and took Little Honda out of the garage. By then, computers in *A's reality* had become necessary tools of research, pressing us to be there more and more frequently. The technology, on our side, was relatively different as the result of the unavailability of petrochemical products. We didn't have personal computers, but our libraries largely made up for the difference, by providing terminals in members' homes. Instead of plastic casings, our monitors and keypads were made of brushed copper and nickel—a far better look!

What were the odds of *the wife* being on our tails? Fairly high, no doubt! So, that was what it came down to for *the Firm*: locating the office and breaching the barrier of our research. It translated into them needing something indispensable to the continuation of their plan, the one item they couldn't get from anyone at the Program: the schematic for what was to replace the system of *fixed bridges*—in other words—my *self-erasables'* recipe.

That recipe was methodological, in that it existed only in the form of teaching. Of course, I had ample papers written about it, but nothing as close as giving anyone a chance at a successful start. Though, I have to admit that in the hands of a skillful, corrupt member, it could potentially have been cracked. Luckily, there were no such members among *designers*, the only ones with enough knowledge to understand the visceral nature of the science. But nothing could have stopped *the Firm* from pointing a gun at my head—or Chance's—though that might not have guaranteed a propitious response.

Again, that didn't change the aura of urgency *the wife* had abruptly brought to our lives. She was well aware I lived in Bayland County from her marriage to John, but she was looking in the other *Bayville*, the one John most likely never visited. Somehow, she knew there were two identical houses across from each other, built after the split; and that was why she was taking images.

Sadly, and conveniently, *the Firm* was walking into a net of its own making. The closer they got, the more we understood what they lacked to destroy us. The *fixed system* was a one passenger deal, with immutable points that necessitated users to travel physically in order to reach any non-system destination; just like public transport—useless beyond stops and stations—in other words: inconvenient past their intended purpose. Even if *the Firm* possessed the science behind the *network*, they knew by now that there was no way to create new *bridges* from it. The template was made redundant during roughly the thirty years that followed 1870. They were stuck with an increasingly obsolete réseau that began showing signs of aging. For unexplained reasons, some of the points started to disappear and reappear randomly, making the crossings dangerous. Nonetheless, *the wife's* proximity indicated that *the Firm* suspected we were in possession of a replacement, and that I was likely the one to supply them with it. Did they just guess, or were they tipped? I started wondering how much *the CEO* got from John via *the wife* about my person. My rapid climb to First-Generation professors had visibly upset my old friend during our reacquaintance at that first party in San Francisco—how long before the whispers of resentment found a willing ear? It might have sounded like self-aggrandizing paranoia, but there was no room for second-guessing the self—all options were good options. The fact remained that *the wife* was seen in town.

— o —

On the day preceding *Three's* arrival in San Francisco for her yearly visit, Chance and I drove the hydromobile along the beautiful stretch that cut through Willits, on our way to pick her up at Pier 29. As I already explained, I would never have thought of replacing those rides with the utilitarian convenience of *bridges*. A drive as beautiful as one flirting with the ancient giants for miles on end was a communion, a reaffirmation that we all had a tie to the Earth, with deep roots into its soil—as metaphorical as these roots may be. We had crossed so many *bridges* over the last few years, that any chance to sit in one of our two vehicles—the other being Little Honda, of course—was a treat beyond mere pleasure, it was borderline orgasmic. Not to mention that nature always had a way of coercing us into one of her secluded areas for some sacred intimacy, as to remind us wherefrom our bodies came and where they would return. In the meantime, everything in between was fair game.

As usual, we stayed at the motel by the long beach. We indulged in an extended walk along the surf before going to bed on the early side. *Three's* ship was scheduled to arrive at 8:00 the next morning.

— o —

It wasn't until the lasts of the passengers had disembarked that we started to worry. It was unlikely that *Three* had boarded the ship! We checked with the desk, to be met with our worst fears. We immediately called her house in South Adelaide: *Three* had left as planned and was thought to have arrived in San Francisco.

The express cruiser from Terra Australis took a week to reach the North Amerikan continent. It was all we had as a window to position her along possible whereabouts. Not much to go by! Short of a freak accident before getting to the ship, *Three* had most likely been abducted. It didn't require much reflecting on our part to conclude that we had a lot to do with it.

——— o ———

23 – THE MISSING OF *THREE*

Three's absurd disappearance was a multifaceted nightmare. Who else but *the Firm* was behind it?! And just when she was on her way to join us! There was a *You-asked-for-it-so-fuck-you!* message stamped in red across a villainy that stank of all bets being off. By the feel of it, *the CEO* was getting antsy.

One of the facets to that nightmare highlighted that by leaving Bayville in too much of a hurry, we would, in all certainty, blow our cover and hand *the Firm* a license to forage through our files. There wasn't a doubt that *the wife* was close to finding the office *bridge*. One of us had to stay behind! It turned out that the Governor didn't mind keeping an eye on the place for a while; which, as usual, indicated that we were on the right track and that we'd better get on with it. Honestly, it was kind of perfect, or—in Program vernacular—meant to be.

— o —

We left on a taxi-boat straight out of Bayville, one of the first vessels adapted to perpetual motion. It was twice as fast as the rapid, getting us to Adelaide in record time. The fact that the trip was costly and traceable provided *the Firm* with all the right tensions, without us giving anything away. If they had expected we would knee-jerk our way into using the office *bridge*, sorry to have disappointed—but I didn't think they were that naïve. Although there was a chance they wanted us in Adelaide so that they could get to the house and raid the office; I hoped in a way that they did, just for the sake of being met by the Governor.

Three's house was abuzz with drama. Her latest husband—*One*, as it turned out, now teaching at the Chapter—and a pair of his students who lived nearby, were busy hypothesizing on the possible causes of her disappearance. All had appeared normal in the preceding days. Chance made it his task to brief the students on the importance of guarding what they knew, as it was from then on a matter of Program Defense best kept confidential. He also cross-referenced their credentials for potential corruptions, but none were found. The students, Caroline and Marz, with *One's* blessings, agreed to join Chance's technical crew—their assignment: to gather all data about *Three's* contacts with suspect individuals over the course of the year.

Within a day's time, Caroline had made a hit, a big one: McKenzie Henderson had left a message on *Three's* personal answerer, asking her to meet about a few irregularities still remaining in the Chapter's paperwork during her tenure as a teacher, just a formality. As we well knew, *the bitch* no longer worked at the department, so what was the catch? Next came Marz's turn to distinguish himself. In record time, he extracted the conversation from traces left in the sound-taker device *Three* took with her to every class. Even though the files had been deleted, most likely to make room, she had had the prescience of bringing it with her to the appointment; an easily concealable item that apparently didn't cross *the bitch's* list of predictable trickery. But then again, Henderson was no longer in a position to serve her old job, so intent was she on pleasing *the CEO*. In fewer words, she had gotten sloppy.

By then, it was obvious who *the CEO's* left and right hands were. What was less so was his reason for choosing *the bitch*. It made sense with *the wife* to a point, but McKenzie Henderson!? She was what one may call, a mind cut with an axe; even her looks gave away something that was put together in a hurry: she was stocky with a distinct asymmetry to the formation of her angles, her face appeared to have collapsed on one side; even her eyes were of noticeably different colours.

The content of the conversation came as no surprise. In spite of the masquerade around the Chapter's paperwork, what she sought was a means to get in to me. *Three* answered in no uncertain terms: *Do your own investigating, and don't ever ask me again to break Chapter protocol!* That was my *Three*—zero nonsense! But I guessed that answer did not satisfy *the CEO*; next came the nasty stuff.

I cannot stress enough how conflicted I became as the result of the kidnapping. Maybe it was *A's world* that was rubbing on me, but I grew fed up with turning in circles by trying my best to play nice. An odd survival instinct was mounting and calling for blood.

I conveyed my emotions to Chance, who understood perfectly well what I meant. He too, had had just about enough of *the Firm's* bullshit, and was ready to raise the antes—we had to make a statement! Defense had located a number of agents stationed on the continent, two in Seaford, Dantes Mansley and Rosalia Gonzales, apparently on duty. It was easy to figure out where they stayed, since it was directly across the street from *Three* and *One's* home. The idea was to uncover the site of the *fixed bridge* that had brought them there and figure out a way to disable it; something we had never done, but which had been on my to-do list for quite a while. The basic concept was to delete all of the old crossings in favour of my *erasables*, but we weren't at that stage yet, which meant that I knew of no specific methodology to erasing a *fixed bridge*.

I had mentioned earlier that some parts of the oldest network had become unstable, so it got me inspired. I took readings between the points that acted out, and the ones that functioned optimally, to establish their differences. I came up with an interesting observation: the most unstable ones had been those closest to *the bridges* created by our travels. The self-erase feature apparently affected the old crossings in such a way that they sought to self-erase as well, which led me to conclude that the two designs were sympathetic. So, what better time and place to test my theory than right then and there, in Adelaide?!

Caroline and Marz found the hot spot. All I had to do was modify the *span code* between there and *A*'s side, by creating a new destination to *Mykineshólmur* in *the Faroe Islands*, land of puffins. After that, we all waited.

It was interesting to witness the debacle when Dantes Mansley tried to use the system and ended up standing there, paralyzed by incomprehension. Soon, the other agent joined in to add her own state of mental freeze to the picture. But then, the bridge came abruptly alive, as our friends—yes, together—were jerked out of their stupor to be sucked into the vortex that took them to their unexpected destination; probably not a place of their liking. What I had theorized had proven me right: the new system was a natural extension of the old—one that could create havoc in *the Firm's* plans. Obviously, restrain was de rigueur, since we needed *Three* alive.

We refrained from fearing our friend had been kidnapped for conditioning. She didn't fit into the usual pattern of *Firm agents* coupling with their preys before the procedure of corruption began. We simply crossed our fingers.

It didn't take long before *the bitch* showed up at the house across the street. She must have known we were in *Three's* home; thus, we prepared for the surprise she had in store for us. But between the two agents' whisk off and Henderson's arrival, Caroline and Marz had visited the place—kept unlocked—and had returned with a log of *the Firm's* recent activities in Adelaide. Yes, agent Rosalia Gonzales had left it behind, likely not expecting she would be wanted in the North Atlantic.

I have to say that I truly relished that moment!

— o —

Yet, my thirst for avengement was far from quenched. *The bitch* was my next target, but not until *Three* was safe. It was then a matter of waiting patiently for her to make a move.

She simply knocked at the door.

It was interesting to witness an act in all of its nakedness. In her case, it wasn't pretty. She was, one might say, fundamentally vulgar, not necessarily in words, but in essence, as in an immutable characterial benchmark bordering on the repulsive.

But there she was, sitting in the chair that had been pulled out for her at the kitchen table. The pretext for her visit was one of neighbourly cordiality, since she had just learned that we were visiting.

I could have killed her right there and then!

She spoke as if she knew nothing of *Three's* whereabouts, or of the fact that we should presently be with her in Bayville. She lied with every breath, insouciant of whether she could be read or not—she didn't seem to care. To her, affront was a way of life. She even went as far as asking where *Three* was, as in a friend wondering what she'd been missing. *One*, who had never met the woman, stood in the middle of the kitchen, befuddled.

In the meantime, Marz and Caroline were busy recording the conversation from the next room. They also understood that operating incognito was part of their job, at which they excelled, and for which they gained my deepest sympathy. In fact, I appreciated the two so much that I started thinking about potential recruitment.

But to Chance and I, McKenzie Henderson's nonsense was wearing thin. She obviously extracted great pleasure at messing with us, but she wasn't good at it. The Prof asked her when she last saw *Three*, an innocent enough question to a person of no reproach, but a loaded one to the wicked. *Oh, perhaps a week or so ago; why do you ask? —Because you're possibly the last one who saw her!* She paused as if to consult a manual then asked, *Why, is she not OK? —No, we assumed she was with you!* Chance struck. *As I said, about a week ago!* she insisted.

It was as far as she went before saying she was sorry for what had happened, and that she would check with her old department. By then we knew where *Three* was. After a few more pleasantries, *the bitch* left straight for *the bridge*. It didn't quite work at first, but then her turn abruptly came to be sent off to the puffin colonies.

Before leaving the subject of *the Faroe Islands*, let us just imagine that the *fixed bridge* out of Adelaide only offered a one-way trip, and that there were no known system points ever connecting that part of the world. The destination was a gift from Janette!

I understand that I might have appeared vindictive at the time, but *the Firm* had tested me to the point of breakage. It wasn't in my nature to seek punitive measures, but dealing with the ills of *A's world* sort of pushed me in that direction; it was part of the rules of adaptation. Also, the *CEO* needed to understand that we were past Program protocol, and by that I meant that we were ready to play according to his rules. At that point, I didn't care anymore about concealing my position—I was a changed woman, ready for the fight.

— o —

Three was in the only place she could possibly have been: with the Governor. First-Generation faculty entities were the foundation of the Program, a group that sat directly under the two highest tiers of responsibility. After a series of increasingly tedious meetings with *the bitch*, *Three* came to understand what was going on, namely that some people were intent on knowing the exact location of my dwellings. She could have called or written, but her rank didn't simply open channels for the sake of attracting eavesdroppers; she had all the intentions of warning me—in a unique way. Instead of the rapid to San Francisco, for which she had already bought a ticket, she voyaged on a different ship to Vancouver and drove down the Pacific to Bayville. All was set to make Chance and me aware of who was on our tails. *One*, Marz, and Caroline were all part of her plan to expose McKenzie Henderson—I would know what to do. I was made aware

176

of it the moment *the bitch* hesitated—there had been no kidnapping. It was a set diversion all along, one intended on upping the odds in the favour of the Program, a message to *the CEO* letting him know he was being watched. Chance and I were no longer alone on the case; we had been joined by *One*, *Three*, and the two students—a rare, partaking move by the Governor.

———— o ————

24 – LATER YEARS WITHOUT *A*

The two systems of *bridges*, which to that point had been limited to Chance and I, and of course, the Governor, were now open to four more entities. We all traveled back to Bayville via one of my *erasables*, to be met by *Three* and the Gov in the office.

The Governor, who routinely introduced prospective students to the Program, showed his sincere appreciation for Caroline and Marz's accomplishments. Without further ado, they were offered teaching positions in Program Defense, pending advanced tutoring by Chance. They were the first professors to be given access to *new bridge design* and a comprehensive view of the old system, with the intension, down the line and with my blessings, of integrating the two into one unique, mutable network *of erasables*—not really a map, but more like a moving gestalt of *path energy*, if that makes any sense.

— o —

Since the rekindling of my connection with *A*, I have been thinking about the threshold that separates us, *character* and *tale-maker*. Whereas a *bridge* may bring us together physically, that *line* simply isn't crossable. The channel of our union is not one of physical nature; it's strictly a soul connection that exists independently from the flesh. As I understood it with the taxi incident, one doesn't necessarily lead to the other, in spite of my impossible sexual attraction to him while in the backseat of his yellow machine. Had he shared the feeling, we would have returned to my motel room without ever considering the consequences. It wasn't the soul that had brought me to the edge of losing control, but my direct connection to that part of myself. *A* was unaware of what I knew and where I operated from; even when he sensed a link, he was in no position to put a name to it.

Never, during the fourteen years of silence, did I wish to find another *character* for my story; it belonged to *A*. I also sensed he had something no-one else possessed: a deeper understanding of what Janette Smyth was made of, a singular thing, even *she* didn't know about herself. There was a mystery surrounding my person I grappled with over the years, the sense that there wasn't enough room in my inner space to contain the essence of who I was. That sensation never left me. I felt both halved and doubled in a disconcerting dance of simultaneously defying balance and seeking to maintain it. In the taxi with *A*, I came closest to breaking out of my skin, like two parts being drawn to the complete being that he was; while *he*, tragically, tried to put a name on a *me* that belonged to a place far removed from the bustle of taxis and city streets, the meeting space from which we could almost reach to touch the other—a delicious illusion—but in which we could never be together in whole, as symmetrical motion would only tear us apart.

— o —

That sense of living in a too-tight-a-suit forced me to evaluate the true meaning of *it was meant to be* in the context of the last years of the eighties, at the time of our return to Bayville from Adelaide. It brought me to imagine where the Program would have been, had I not been pulled in the direction of *the Firm*. It seemed to have all started at the time of my first solo crossing into *Bayville*. In spite of my vulnerability, I felt stronger than I had been in a long time. But I recall that it was also a period when I perceived the Program as being in a kind of reboot mode. My first trip south to *Longville* was the maker by which my attention was caught by a nuanced quality about my life that wasn't there before: the *subliminality* that my renewed sense of balance was borne of new purpose—that of taking charge of *bridge-building*, a choice that led me straight to *the Firm*. I was conscious the Governor put me to the task; it was also when the *it-was-meant-to-be* part came into frame.

Life is always on the edge of reinventing itself. In 1985, it couldn't have been a truer maxim when I felt that I had stepped over that edge in more ways than one. If I hadn't followed the course that lay before me, there would have been little chance for the Program to have ever heard of *the Firm*, and for Defense to have been created. That time was akin to a change of mind on the part of an indescribable deep self. Something in the universe had slammed on the brakes just in time to take the other road; but all along, it seemed to have been accompanied by a little voice in my head, not as much a voice as it was a vision; and not a much a vision as it was a calling. On that occasion, it was almost *not* meant to be.

— o —

I am never going to be able to say that I eventually forgot about *A*, but by 1992, right after the Program switched gears into action, my life became fully absorbed by the plan of dismantling *the Firm* and exposing the

CEO. The team, as it was called from then on, and composed of the six of us, plus Defense as the main strategic instrument, was ready for its first steps into tactical offensive. We chose to begin with blocking access to some of the known *fixed bridges*, in pretty much the same way I had sent *the bitch* and the other two agents on forced vacation in *the Faroes*. But in order to send and forever lock the entire organization in *A's world*, we had to keep *the Firm's* more established pathways open, hence the wall at which we came. They knew what we were up to and there was no way they would fall for the trap. By existing simultaneously on both sides of *bridges* we could not close, and controlling a portion of *tale-makers* whom we couldn't prevent from corrupting data, other than pretty much ruining their minds by *unplugging* them—something that had never been done—*the Firm* technically maintained a distinct advantage over us.

So much for an offensive!

But before they caught up with us, we had managed sending a number of their agents to locations difficult to leave; and frankly, at that point, we didn't care whether they survived their environment or not.

One contemplated option was to corrupt their operatives, equivalently to what they had done to us. But that required extremely skilled members capable of faking a weakness for corruption, in order to draw in agents and snare them inside relationships. But it was dangerous. Some volunteered, although it was a lot to demand of anyone.

For a period of two years, we froze the admission process and shut down some of the Chapters in order to regroup—something akin to a victory for the *CEO*, as we observed a brief laxing of *the Firm's* operation. But he couldn't be that stupid, although the man's character still had to be defined beyond inconclusive analysis.

The stroke of genius emerged from team Caroline and Marz who came up with the idea of tricking the *fixed bridges*, so that once agents crossed into *A*'s reality, their return paths would be secretly rerouted to terminal points in ours—a system of one-way fares that was to lock *the Firm* on our side rather than the other. By terminal points, we meant places where those agents would find themselves fully disconnected from each other, and consequentially, of no use to *the CEO*.

The only drawback to that plan was the potential upping of *the Firm's* determination to destroy the Program with an all-out offense; by that, I mean, random kidnapping, torture, and murder—words which I would prefer didn't belong to this story. But it was an option worth considering if we were meant to show progress. The concept was to cross into *A's* on a *fixed bridge* and affix an overlay for the return destination. Did I ever mention these old crossways could only connect with their mirror locations on the other side, unlike *erasables*? In other words, the *fixed system* was made of two identical maps, one in each world. By tricking the *bridges* on *A's side* into recognizing a different image on ours, the two maps would essentially come apart. It was, in essence, a risky hybridization of the old and new, but I trusted *the Firm* wouldn't make any sense of it.

— o —

The *CEO* was a paradox; his counterpart lived and died in his own time in *A's world*. We already speculated he got caught in between points when the Governor shut

182

the *fixed system* for nearly sixty years. Upon his release, he was condemned to staying where he belonged—with us. For the sake of clarity, none of us had doubles on the other side, and if we had, we wouldn't have been permitted to cross—a simple law of quantum physics. In the case of *the CEO*, and in spite of his displacement in time, he was still very much on a parallel line—shifted as it were—with the self that once lived in *A's world*. So, in simple terms, no crossing for him! I hope I am making myself clear.

The point was to expose *the CEO* and *the Firm's* vulnerabilities as much as it was possible, with the aim of finding where to strike. Likely, all of their agents had been recruited from *A's reality* by *the wife*; but we didn't have the foggiest idea whence said-wife came. We simply assumed she too got caught in the *fixed system*, while accidentally crossing from *A's side*; in which case, it remained undetermined how the two met. It was conceivable that within the confines of being locked between points, they ended up existing intimately. All we knew was that she could travel freely between worlds, which meant she didn't have a counterpart. Our calculations put her at having been born between 1870 and 1900—after the split but before the shutdown of the *bridges*—most likely, in the upper seventies and lower eighties of the 19th century. She and *the CEO* were essentially polar opposites.

— o —

I would much prefer to forego the technical descriptions in favour of a lither prose, but my story didn't turn out to be what I had in mind as a youth. I was a butterfly then, blessed with having exceptional parents and exquisite surroundings. I need to stress that play has not totally left me in favour of hardness. It's important to find balance when weights are disproportionably apportioned. *One*, *Three*, Chance, and I had made it a point of lightening up in regard to the Program; too many times had we let it enter the heart and allowed for it to steal a place that belonged to self-love and the songs of birds. That being said, we still had a job to do.

— o —

We monitored each of the known agents and observed which ones of the *bridges* they used most. As I said earlier, those points were a one-person-at-a-time deal, so they couldn't take anyone with them, and certainly not their Program mates, since the last thing on their minds was to give these souls access to the *fixed system*. We figured that if we proceeded with timely restrain and by hitting *bridges* far apart from each other, *the Firm* might not catch up with us until some damage was inflicted. In the meantime, Defense had created a rehabilitation center to receive *widowed* members; though it remained unclear what the definition of *rehabilitation* consisted of. The creation of a quarantine area would have been a more accurate interpretation for it.

And so, we began. It took two years and the loss of sixty-two *Firm* agents before *the CEO* acted. By then, we were in position to guard our members. We lost a few of those who had made their silent allegiance to *the Firm*, but we had no wish to protect them; it was much too late for them to redeem themselves. I thought of John and his fate, of his proximity to one of the fiercest agents to seek doom upon the Program. I resigned myself to losing him to her blade. But the game wasn't over yet; no decisive victory had been made. Yes, we had disabled a fifth of the *bridges* and made a statement, but they still had the bulk of their forces teamed to a plethora of *tale-makers*—some we hadn't tallied yet—and we were left with a hallful of irreversibly corrupted members with no place to go.

Marz suggested showing those souls the way across *fixed bridges*; thus locking them on the other side; perhaps they would eventually find their mates there. We looked at each other as if he had lost his mind, but we soon saw a mix of humour and relief in the concept. As a result, fifty-one ex-members were sent their sweet ways into *A's world*. Maybe they would go crazy, or maybe not, but at least, they were given a chance to exist with their dignity intact. It wasn't subtle, but it solved one of our biggest dilemmas. Each step forward was a victory.

— o —

By 1995, Chance had left the Bayville office to return to Monterey. We had spent a long time together, becoming more and more of an item. We never admitted to it though; as a matter of fact, we seldom discussed it— we weren't meant to be attached to definitions. But I have to be honest with my feelings; his departure broke my heart. My vow of independence had no value left to it; it was a mockup unfit for the presses of reality. I had fooled myself into believing that strength was defined by the resolve of never seeking anyone for support; it simply wasn't true. To the contrary, strength was determined by the ability to let someone in and be let in. I had never allowed myself to contemplate that I was in love with Chance; I loved him like I loved Little Honda, a pathetic

185

admittance to material love, but a total blackout on the fundamental nature of the unconditional form. I deeply needed Chance to stay by me, yet I stubbornly refused to acknowledge that yearning—it was perceived as a weakness. What a fool!

We saw each other a few times after his move, but something had been broken; namely, I broke both our hearts. He became tired of waiting for me to open up and say, *I love you*, like lovers say, *I love you,* and you feel all of your senses come to life. There was play, which was always welcome, but never was there a moment that stopped time, with the two of us looking each other in the eyes, and saying the dreaded, *I love you, Chance*; *I love you, Janette*. I never allowed for that space to exist. We came close, but I chose to escape, ignoring what I was running away from.

— o —

With Chance leaving, so were Caroline and Marz gone from my life. They had a formidable team to build on. It was another heartache that had brushed a coat of dullness to my reality. Alone, I started to think of *A*.

From the moment he was gone, I feared I had lost him for good. The times I had tried to reach him had left me with a sense of doom looming ahead of his person. The destruction of art, blood stains on the crime scene, and the knife of ruin—in spite of them mixing well— formed an alliance that could only spiral into the bowels of Hell. I never sought to figure out what came of that relationship, for I had determined by then that there was no place for us to coexist beyond the line that separated us—*character* and *tale-maker*—at the level of the soul.

186

A's absence from our meeting place didn't add up to joining the *it-was-meant-to-be* axiom. The lack of resolve at one end, and the ludicrousness of seeing my story blown to the wind at the other, lingered in life's heap of the relinquished, never truly discarded, but not meant to be reconsidered either. It was just there, neglected; another item that ceased to be seen.

The role of the lone wolf was at odds with my sense of loneliness; I had grown accustomed to company, and while I relished the thought of finding peace among my things, in my place, I couldn't bear the silence. And so, I moved the operation to the office in *Bayville*, choosing to live amid the sound of sirens and exhaust fumes instead. I no longer cared about the house on my side; there was nothing left in it for *the Firm* to find.

— o —

I spent nearly two years there without ever returning to my old world. I had gotten so accustomed to *Bayville* that I grew to love the city. I finally broke out of the shield and made friends, very good ones. Not all was corrupt in *A's* world, and whether it was so as the result of the Program's influence or not, I could not tell. Surely with what had been happening with *the Firm*, I didn't think we could accomplish much in terms of healing the place. Rather, it seemed that it was my world that needed the care.

I hoped to bump into *the wife*, get to know her, understand what made her tick. It was of no consequence to me if she knew where I lived—we no longer had anything to hide from each other—and perhaps, she didn't care anymore either. The only thing she would

187

want out of me was my knowledge of *the erasables*, but I didn't think *the CEO* had caught up with it yet, since only seven people were aware of its existence. But *the wife* never showed up in my circle. It was possible that she didn't expect me to have moved into her world; after all, members of the Program had no knowledge of the *bridges*, fixed or not. On the other hand, *the Firm* wouldn't have showed interest in me and Chance if they hadn't suspected us to have crossed on many occasions.

Most likely, my moving into *A's* world was a victory for *the CEO*—what better way to win than convincing a senior Program member that the other side was worth defecting to? If they had watched me all along, two years without going back was warrant to a full turn around—I was the prized item, worn-out and exiled, *head designer of tale-making* with a dead *character* and no story left to tell. I was no longer of interest to them.

— o —

To be forgotten suited me well. Even the Governor hadn't sought to connect. Chance could have found me if he had wanted to, but as I said; he had been tired of waiting, and me being gone was nothing more than another expression of the emotional distance I had wedged between us. It suited me well because it forced me to take a good look at myself and my role in the Program. I had offered *tale-making* which was now jeopardized by corruption, and *bridge-building* held captive by extraordinary circumstances. No other branch of the Program had been affected by *the Firm* in such a way my two contributions were. It was as if I had been made the primary target. Wasn't it through John, after all,

188

that I became aware something was wrong? Of course, nothing could be worse than a pathetic case of personal projection, but I was trained to look at the larger picture—no part was ever taken for granted.

The CEO and I only had a short history that started in the late eighties—no reason I should think I was the center of attention—it anyone was, it would have to have been the Governor. But still, I felt there was something I couldn't quite put my finger on.

— o —

One day, while coming out of the food co-op, I saw a man getting in an old, red pick-up truck and leaving the car lot. My heart jumped in my chest; I swore it was *A*. He was older, definitely not as healthy or good looking as he had been back in San Francisco, but there was still an aura about his presence that couldn't lie. So, he was alive after all! But why did he choose to disconnect?

I kept on forgetting *A* didn't sense my presence the way I did his. I was his sacred feminine—he was my *character*. He chose to put his trust in me, while I used him to send messages across. Of course, I loved him, but if he loved me in return, it was a much more personal form of love, a self-love dependent on the faith there was actually someone inside that whispered, protected, and listened to the sound of pain. He left me because the sacred feminine had become unreliable, distrustful... even dangerous. I was too selfish about what I needed from him to acknowledge that my love for him wasn't a reciprocation of his—I was desperate for his love because the success of my work at *tale-making* was dependent on the strength of our rapport. I had failed to heed the warnings of my own collapse when we almost lost each other the first time around. I chose to forget how much he meant to me, the same way I chose to ignore Chance's heart. Of course, I had nothing to do with *A's* choices in relationships, those followed by betrayals, lies, blackmail, and mean-spiritedness. But I could have been more present and supportive when I sensed his energy fraying under the duress. Instead, I kept on feeding him a story that had little to do with his life, expecting that, one day, he would put it into words. *Goodness, Janette, what took you to mismanage a connection so vital to the platform on which you birthed your brainchild?!* The thought struck me like a whip—*tale-making* was in trouble because I had been negligent, while carrying that very negligence through my teaching: that of not treating *the character* as a part of my own, of not considering the intrinsic symbiosis of that fragile and precious connection.

— o —

It wasn't totally coincidental that within days of seeing *A* in the car park, he showed up at the threshold again. The year was 2000, the 2nd of July to be exact.

——— o ———

190

25 – GATEKEEPER

A and I have never been better. The night following my sighting at the lot, I made the decision to return to my house in Bayville. The Governor was waiting for me in the office. He informed me that I had been added to the group of *overseers* and that pending the fixing of my issues with *tale-making*, I could return to teaching the course. *Bridge-building* was put on the back burner until further notice, but I was free to continue with my personal use of *erasables* and figure out the better ways to integrate the old and new systems into one.

As usual, the Governor knew something I didn't, and honestly, it started to eat at me. I wasn't even sure why I had been promoted to *overseer* when I did nothing but shun the Program to wait for *the wife* to show up. I assumed that spending two years in a world to which I didn't belong and finding comfort in it, qualified as a particularly unique approach to building lateral awareness. But I wasn't clear on how it could benefit the Program. The one advantage I possessed was a practically innate understanding of life there, notwithstanding that my fears of it were forever erased. As it turned out, it was a lot more important that I could have imagined—I had become a permanent resident of both worlds, and as the Governor put it, I qualified as the official gatekeeper.

There was a lot in fourteen years I needed to update *A* with, as the result of which, much was omitted due to plain forgetfulness. So many details about how we went on countering the *CEO's* attacks on the students and faculty; how Chance, team Caroline/Marz, Program

Defense, and little me traced and tallied the corrupt *tale-makers* and their agents; volumes after volumes of tedious data about investigative work, statistics, agents' profiles, predictions, strategy—none of it important for this story, but nonetheless worth mentioning—that were filled, encrypted, and eventually filed in the Straßburg Chapter's vaults. All that needed to be forwarded was the fact that, during that time, we had slowed *the Firm* in its tracks and prevented irreversible damage to be done to the Program. The fact that *the wife* and McKenzie Henderson hadn't been seen in years was indicative *the Firm* had suffered a setback. Naturally, it was assuming *the bitch* had eventually found her way back from *the Faroes*. Based on suspect Corbyn's latest follow-up, we had good reasons to believe she was around—she simply had run out of excuses to pester me.

— o —

So now, I can technically say that I am up to date with *A*. I'm also up to date with the way I must handle my relationship with him. It's obvious he now lives on his own, and I can tell it's for the better. I sense a rebirth in the making; actually, there is a form of death happening as well—a part of him is dying, not just figuratively, but I mean, a physical death, as if a worn-out body were being replaced by a new one. Hard to explain, really—like he is two, as I feel I am two most of the time, except one of me isn't dying, or is she? At any rate, it's quite miraculous, especially since he seems to be aware of the process. It's a good time for me to put my thoughts to action and give *A* all the female support he needs, for it seems he tends to fall back into recurring patterns and it can't happen this time around. Hopefully, he won't fall for the energy that I sense is presently purveying to that weakness, something sensual and quasi-wicked, not necessarily mean or dangerous, but definitely lusting for the kind of attention tied to old, unquenched longings. He desires to fix the unfixable, and every time, he loses a life in the process. So, I stay near him to the best of my abilities—I need him, he needs me—what else am I to do? I might as well admit it to myself: I'm in love with him.

— o —

I was first under the impression that the Governor and *the CEO* were archenemies, but in reality they weren't, for the latter only showed up after he came loose of the system of *fixed bridges*, aged as he was before being caught in it. The Governor is an ageless entity, while *the CEO* is mortal and nearing the end of his useful life. He's somewhere in my world and it's my intention to meet him before he dies, if I'm not already too late. *The wife*, even though she was born in the late eighteen hundreds, is still plenty young and most likely in charge, but I am somewhat concerned about her plans, especially since seeing John at that gallery a month or so ago, all aged and prematurely worn out.

It's hard for me to muster the whys of *the CEO* and *the wife* wanting to target the Program as the cause of their predicament, though I understand how they came to make that choice. Sure, the Governor shut down *the bridges*, but how did they know? Did he advertise his presence and his role in the system, while announcing that they were trapped for the next sixty years? If so, I can understand their anger, but there has to be something else,

193

and I don't think I will get it from the Governor. So now, I'm all the more resolute to find *the CEO* and get his version of the story. Let's see how logic serves!

— o —

The hydromobile rolls out of the garage with a gentle purr.

When I visited my parents in Junction Station upon my return from *Bayville*, I offered for them to move to the house. For the first time ever, they showed interest, only I couldn't force them to sell the farm, or prevent dad from feeding the chicken every morning. And so he went bright and early, rain or shine, in his mini hydro. They agreed to rent the house to the son of a trusted friend, who promised he would tend to the gardens and bring fresh veggies to the house. Mom was happy with the arrangement—she was ready to become a city gal!

I pull out the auto because I'm on my way to San Francisco. Chance and I are meeting there to discuss the option of starting a new partnership. Yes, another lesson for Janette on the way—a hard one, for which I find myself overtaken with emotions.

I had been missing the three-road drive down to the big city with its midway rest stop in Willits. In *A's world*, I had taken Little Honda a few times down the freeway to do research in the Bay Area and Silicon Valley. They have computers with the internets, which we don't have here, but it comes at a cost. Based on personal observations, I see potential for much corruption down the line, even as far as the spread of propaganda and the manipulation of social behaviour. In the wrong hands, their internets could become a dangerous weapon.

But I'm here in the present, driving past Longville, flashing on the native man's warning, in the sister town, long ago. I wonder what he had read in my aura that had stirred darkness within him. What had he meant by *you should go home!*? How did he know I wasn't home? But it's just a thought that goes away.

I have not seen Chance since a few months after he went back to Monterey—I am so anxious! And why am I anxious? *For Heaven's sake, Janette, you have known the man for over twenty years!* I am guilty of having betrayed the love between us, that's why! And that's also why I don't know that man, the man behind the heart—because I'm afraid of the woman behind my own! *Calm down, you haven't committed a wrong, it's just some poorly justified fear; you're overacting your emotions!* That's the scenario in my head. I have no choice but to let it run its course—I'm sure I'll be fine!

— o —

We—the hydro and I, that is—stop in Willits as planned. I feel much better with some food in my stomach. I can't ignore the fact that the market fares, on both sides, have gotten so much more interesting. In *A's*, the organic movement has become unstoppable. Of course, in ours, old-school farming never left us in the first place; that's why we have no such term as *organic*— not to mention the word makes little sense since it also means *containing the chemical element carbon*, and that lots of dangerous chemicals have carbon in them. I like *conventionally-farmed* much better, but conventional farming in *A's world* allows the use of chemical fertilizers and pesticides. That's what I mean by corruption!

Anyway, I'm glad for them that organic food and commonsense are being recognized. I would like to point that *le mouvement biologique* started in France at the time of the reopening of the *fixed bridges*—coincidence? Maybe, but one never knows with the Governor.

Chance and I are to meet at the motel by the beach. This time we have booked separate rooms. I get to mine way ahead of his arrival, which gives me plenty of an opportunity to take a walk on the sand. I remember when we sat here on one of our first trials with *bridging* sister points. That day, we had rooms on both sides and made love in each of them. The memory is both humorous and discomforting. Play is not a bad thing when we need not involve the heart, but it can become an unhealthy habit when used as a means of escape.

— o —

I didn't tell Chance, when we last spoke, that I intended on locating *the CEO*, who I believe resides in the San Francisco Bay Area. I shall keep it to myself until I determine whether we have a team or not. That being said, I am drawn to face the truth about that mysterious man. Honestly, he may not exist at all, since he is a speculated entity I created during my early research on *the Firm*. He could be John D. Rockefeller, or not, or just a projection on my part as a means to deny *the wife* the title of villainess-in-charge. But today, I start from the premise there is such an individual, and I'm fully intent on stopping by his place to say hi.

One may say that, in my story, I speak amply of a man that might not even be real. But remember that I tend to proceed from the standpoint that something is there before proven otherwise. Right or wrong, it always leads somewhere. Without it, *the Firm* could well be on its way to destroy the Program, and we wouldn't know the first thing about it. I can viscerally feel *the CEO's* presence, hence why he is a vital part of the case.

— o —

Chance is late—something to do with a slide on the coastal highway. It works for me because I feel like procrastinating about meeting again. My time in *A's world* has informed me that the term for a person such as myself is *chicken shit*—not too subtle, but to the point. I could be elated about seeing Chance again, but no, I find solace in his lateness instead, while he's probably doing his best to get here on time. You know I'm really nervous when I'm all over the map! In all seriousness though, I'm anxious to see him. Scared? yes, but nervous with excitement. I promised to behave, but at the same time I'm afraid I might blow it, like in a bad dream. *Blow what, Janette, what's to blow?* Here we go again—the pleasures of being two in my own mind! Good thing I'm no longer prone to existential angst... But I hear a voice outside my door—there's a knock.

— o —

It's odd; someone I've never met but who claims to know me, stops by to ask permission to borrow a moment of my time. His name: Anatole, a French man with good manners reminiscent of the Governor's. I oblige. As it turns out, he's a poet, a journalist, and a well respected novelist; an ideal *tale-maker's character* if I

197

may say so. He's also not of this world, and even more extraordinarily, not of this time, judging by the accoutrement. Actually, he knows of me from the Program, to which I am anxious to learn which Chapter he's supposed to have studied at. *The Lyon Chapter, from 1865 to 1868*, he says. That shuts me up for a minute while the gears in my head come dangerously close to unmeshing. In spite of his goatee and handlebar mustache, he looks rather young—thirty something perhaps. *How are you here?* I ask. *Bridge*, he says. Now, I am really spinning! *Bridge from where?* —*Paris, 1870.* When I ask him the reason for his visit, he gets up and simply says, *Vous comprendrez, au revoir !* He's gone.

Earth to Janette! What exactly just happened?! A French man from the eighteen hundreds, novelist, journalist, and poet, shows up at my door in 2000 San Francisco, bridging time to an erasable *space point* Chance and I created over a decade ago—OK, I give up!

I have never factored time in, beyond a few glitches in both *fixed* and *new bridges*; and wham, comes Anatole reminding me of what I have grossly overlooked! One way to cure my apprehension of seeing Chance— now I need him desperately!

I'm not going to speculate—it is what it is, a game-changer for certain. *Bridges*, *fixed* or not, can access various time periods; it's just a matter of figuring out how to do it. It's also another twisted item to add to the case. So, in which Bay Area am I going to find *the CEO*—a past or a future one? Thanks, Anatole!

To this point, I've never considered the Program to have existed as it does in its present form: Chapters, students, and a faculty composed of professors, *designers*, *overseers*, and the Governor. But according to Anatole's few words, the same setup existed in Lyon, nearly a century and a half ago. I knew the Program went back very far in time, but I imagined it to have been more like a secret society than a proper academy. But why Anatole, and why now, just as I'm about to reunite with Chance? As usual with what smells of old musty offices and mothballed suits, it must be important.

— o —

Chance looks exhausted, although he's pretty much he same as I have always known him—ageless. We hug without touching, the way people do, mechanically, when their minds are somewhere else—which shouldn't be the case here, but it is. Sure, I expected more, but apparently, not today. I resign myself to eating my slice of humble pie and keeping it at that. We're meeting in a coffee shop a block from the motel; nothing as intimate as one of our rooms. I wonder if Chance's serious demeanour is an act of old resentment, or if he has given himself to cynicism. I find neither reason conducive to healthy teamwork. I just hope he's feeling the way I feel, a bit weathered by the strong winds of life, but quick to pick up when things settle. Today was alright until the road slide and Anatole's visit, I guess.

We go over the work accomplished at both his end and mine, the progress made by Defense, the dwindling in agent activity, the disappearance of *the wife* and *the bitch*, et cetera. After a while, it all looks oh too simple, too easy—time to bring Anatole in the picture!

At first, Chance looks at me as if I were crazy, but when he realizes I'm dead serious, he comes up with the only thing the male mind can muster on such occasion:

199

What the fuck?! Yes, Chance, what the fuck?!—no need for mental process, no verb, it's not even a question, but I give you the question mark anyway; yours is just an exclamation as if something heavy had fallen on your foot: *Ouch!* In all fairness, it's not that much worse than my previous *OK I give up!*, but at least, it didn't come out as a grunt.

My thoughts try to put order to the mental chaos. I look Chance in the eyes—*Something's the matter?* He looks back, absentmindedly—*Nothing to do with you!* I am relieved, who would have imagined? *Care to share?* OK, not now, I understand.

So, yes, Anatole came to visit, a century and a half in his future, with a message contained in his very presence: the fact we forgot to include time as the other half of space. Oddly, it also appears that upon linking the two motels on that pivotal day years ago, Chance and I created both *fixed* and *erasable sets of points*! At any rate, if *the Firm* knows, we have been played all along. We try to persuade ourselves that they don't know; that Anatole *is* a Chapter member with intrinsic knowledge of the network, while *the CEO* was merely caught off-guard in a place he didn't comprehend and might still not fully understand. When in doubt, rationalize!

In the end, the best way to know is to figure out how to use the *bridges* the way Anatole and, most assuredly, the Governor do. I suggest that we visit 1870 using the place the Frenchman came and left from. Chance reminds me that, years ago, said *point* led to a sleazy motel a block or so south of here. *So what, Chance, is that a rule?* But I keep it to myself. I pressure him into accepting it is the same spot used by Anatole. We're talking adjacent rooms—easy enough for him to

disappear before I had a chance to catch up. The Prof isn't
fully convinced, since he still believes the visitor accessed
an *erasable point* from a *fixed* one, but he doesn't fight
the notion off either. It's also his room and there is no
danger of him being lured into mine, if you get my drift!

— o —

Chance brings to my attention that 1870 was the
year of the split. Although I already know that, his point
is that there wasn't an *A's world* back then; that date
belongs to a common past, accessible from both sides. It
makes a lot of sense. In turn, I suggest that by using an
erasable, we might prevent an unwanted awakening of
the Firm into the knowledge of the time factor, in case
they'd be looking. Finally, Chance turns to me with the
kind of intensity I came to love during our years working
together: *What if they already know but haven't found a
way around it; and what if they're also aware we haven't
yet figured it out; are you certain about the safety of the
erasables? —They may speculate, but those, they for sure
don't know anything about!* I counter, which roughly
translates into, *What are we waiting for?!*

— o —

As the official gatekeeper, I am under pressure to
perform, so I'm not telling Chance about method. I am
already judge and audience, since there always seems to be
two of me anyway; no need to crowd the field. Anatole is
from 1870 Paris; I imagine a suggestive decor of
cobblestone streets, carriages and the sound of horseshoes
hitting the pavers—a day wrapped in the smell of manure,

201

urine, shoe polish, mold, leather, spice, and perfume. *Hang on, Chance, I almost have it!* And there we are, in an office, facing Anatole and the Governor. They look at each other in approval—I guess we're on time.

— o —

Chance's stare begs to ask, *How did you do that?* I wouldn't be able to explain; it's something I only minimally thought of, an ability that probably has been with me all along, and which, as they say, comes in its own time and space, and as it turns out, should be in the year 1870. *Didn't I just say it's been with me for a while!?* Since I am the gatekeeper, I shall content myself with seeing the humour of the situation in private.

We're being asked to take a seat, but neither of us feels like sitting. I engage by enquiring about the reasons for us being expected in this part of the world without as much as enough time to slip into something more fashionable. Both Anatole and the Governor ignore my attempt at relaxing the absurdity of the moment. A congratulatory reception would have been nice, but I might be expecting too much out of these two. The Governor does indeed say that I chose well by utilizing the *erasable platform*, as only a few of the *fixed bridges* are presently secure, namely, the two privately used by our hosts, including the one in and out of the motel—*ha, didn't I say!*—but not for much longer, according to Anatole the poet. In other words, we're being informed that starting with now, the *fixed system* is no longer needed by the Program—my *erasables* being the official replacements—and that complete shutdown should be expected as soon as ready. *How are you going to travel? I* ask, since I believe the Governor has never used an *erasable*, and it looks like Anatole wouldn't know one if it were in front of him. *As you have already noticed, your erasable became fixed long enough for your visitor to come through; you will figure it out! Thank you for your work; it isn't too early for a completed version of the new system!* answers the Governor. Yes indeed, I tend to not take credit when credit is due! *How is it being a writer without a tale-maker?* I probe Anatole unabashedly. He smiles for the first time. *No tale-maker? Who do you think came up with the idea of getting the United States to join France against Prussia?* I knew it!

— o —

As usual, the Governor isn't into sharing what he has on his mind. I ask Anatole how he sees the denouement of the conflict: *Alone, a French defeat brings on catastrophic consequences; but a Prussian victory over both the United States and France steers the world away from the worst. —As in our world? —That is what I have seen,* he says. *How do you know it will change the course of history in such a way? —It is a gamble, an outcome as opposed to another; I had a glimpse when I visited; it looked alright. —Is it the way it is intended? — It depends on what happens with your case.* With that, he excuses himself and leaves the room. The Governor lets us know our time is up. *You should be able to find your way back!* he says, before exiting as well.

That leaves Chance, who hasn't spoken much, in a quasi-catatonic state. *Time to go!* I say. He snaps out of it, *What about that, what about that—what about that!* Correction: he hasn't quite snapped out of it. I take us back to the motel, proposing we meet later to talk about it. He's OK with that, apologizing for still being caught in the spell of the visit. *You'd better get used to it, Chance!* I think to myself. We each go to our rooms, still not touching.

— o —

As you can see, we have a complicated situation. Well, I am left with one. *It depends on what happens with your case...* That's kind of enigmatic, considering I'm unsure which direction the case is taking, that is, if it's moving at all. We've reached the stage at which we can disable the *fixed bridges*—I have no idea how it's done, but the Governor knows—so that *Firm agents* get stuck wherever they are, without the means to travel within their realities, or cross between ours and theirs. Deprived of *the bridges*, they are technically defeated. Unless, of course, they're satisfied with where they stand and have no need for them anymore. That would be very unfortunate for the Program! Ideally, we want the agents to return to *A's world* where they belong. *The wife* remains a mystery as to which side she should spend her final days, but personally, I prefer she stays with *the CEO* on ours. It's just a matter of being able to keep an eye. As I have said, I've come to love the other reality as much as I do my own; I don't want anymore harm done to it by the crazies of this Earth, whichever side they originate from. I want them to go back to their holes and shut the fuck up. May they swim in cologne! It's bad enough to live amid the irresponsible acts of the corporate mindset, but who needs outside fanatics to tell the world that greed, toxicity, and lies are good for you? *A's world* doesn't need that

204

anymore than we do. Wouldn't it be wonderful if we could have *bridges* between the two and cross without the fear we might never be able to return—sister realities, paralleling each other, sharing their exquisite differences? With healing work and perseverance, it's totally possible, and that's what the Program is all about!

It was inevitable that a split would occur at the insertion of the US/France pact. The outcomes were only foreseeable to a point, but it was clear that the Governor saw the rise of the oil industry as a blemish on future history, and possibly, an irreversible course into darkness. It's obvious to me that the reopening of the *fixed bridges*—and of the Chapters after that—stemmed from the intent to bring the two worlds back together at some hypothetical point in time. Imagine an *1870* of the future if you can, as a cross-point of reunification. For the sake of it, let's call it the year 2070. Sounds like a goal!

— o —

Before I get back to Chance and contemplate the details of where we stand as a team, I let my mind drift towards *A*. *A* is totally into the plot. Not only does he embrace what I feed him, but he marvels at the discovery of these inner worlds, (paradoxically, only inner to him.) He knows the information isn't just the fruit of his vibrant imagination, for he has long understood that there is a place from which to observe that exists at the perfect intersection of mind and soul. He sees what he sees, hears what he hears, and trusts that egocentric values do not shape the experience. It's a rare thing indeed, but it can also be a lonely place. At this point, I believe that our relationship is on an exponential climb. I feel blessed.

205

OK, back to Chance! For now he's in his room, not sulking, but one could be fooled. The man is stressed and I should do something about it. If I'm not responsible for his mood, as he says, perhaps I should make myself responsible for making him feel better. I get out and knock on his door. He lets me in with a corner smile that indicates he might be ready to share what's been eating him. He confesses that he and Alice have been seeing each other behind Max's back for a number of years until they got caught. Max was deeply hurt, and now Alice wants out. Typical, but I understand the pain. *So, you wanted her all for yourself! What happened to that wonderful ménage à trois (or à quatre, when you wanted me to join in,) you professed was the Dharma of sexual ecstasy?* I refrain from saying. Sometimes, I wonder how the Program failed at making us less pathetic. I always thought of Chance as a pillar of strength: masculinity exemplified through an immutable law that only males possessed. But here we are, his pride in a puddle because he didn't get to have his cake and eat it too, as they say in *A's world*. But I'm being extremely critical, which I hope sheds light on my own weaknesses. I'm not in the business of fooling myself, for I know too well that my ever-so-playful deriding of Chance's heartbreak is nothing more than my own fear of facing the music vis-à-vis emotional reality. So, I rise to the occasion and offer Chance a back rub. I get a predictable response, but it hurts all the same: *It's never again going to be what it was between us; you understand that, Janette?* I've never been a fan of sentences composed of statements and questions; they always reek of condescension, so if he keeps on with the attitude, I'm going to revert to calling him the Professor. I give him one day to get his act

together before the hydro and I head north. It's funny—
and yet not—how you never can get enough of someone's
love one day and feel like running away the next. Right
now, I want nothing to do with his mood; I find it
manipulative, and frankly, way below him. *Let me know if
you change your mind!* I close his door and aim for the
beach. I just want to be alone for a while.

— o —

We do these superhuman things, like crossing *time
and space bridges*, yet our humanity at its least dignified
never seems to part from us. Oftentimes, the two qualities
grow, leaving a widening divide in their midst. The
thought is discomforting. I want so much to step out of
these patterns of nitpicking and sentimental sniveling. I
take my shoes off, straighten my spine, and hit the water.
It's ice cold, but I need to chill my core, feel my body
through all the warnings. The time has come for *Janette
the gatekeeper* to get back to her labour of love—the
Program. If Chance feels like joining, all the better; if not,
destiny is a big place and I wish him luck.

— o —

26 – FASHION SHOW

We're driving back to Bayville; Chance is with me. We took off in the early morning. The Prof knocked at my door in the middle of the night to snuggle in bed next to me. We didn't have sex, didn't need to, the comfort was all that was required. We grabbed coffees to go and headed immediately out of town. We didn't even discuss the main reason for meeting; that was all part of a silent understanding, which could have fooled me yesterday. But as I said, human nature prevails—the good and the pitiful—through our greatest deeds.

I have spoken of it before; our Golden Gate Bridge isn't as glamorous as the one in *A's San Francisco*. If I could change one thing, I would swap the two. There are other landmarks that are missing in our world, like the Chrysler and the Transamerica Buildings, all of that dizzying architecture that reaches towards the sky in quasi-phallic symbols of wealth and power. Our structures are shorter and more spread out; streets and creeks run through them. Some of the oldest are often part of the new ones, and of course, plants of all kinds grow on top and out of them. But I'm off-topic.

It's a perfect day for driving, so we opt for the coastal route. It's longer, but who would want to miss the exhilarating beauty of the Pacific, with kilometres on end of farmland and ancient redwoods groves running like fingers amid the hills a short distance to the east?

It's also a good opportunity to set the mood for what needs to be discussed between us: the job and our broken relationship.

We settle for fixing the relationship as we go. We are changed people in need to adapt to new selves first; at least, we get the importance of the point.

The job is ill-defined; it always seems to start that way, sticks and stones. Chance is still in charge of Defense, but Caroline and Marz, who have moved up to head multiple departments, are running the operation in his absence. So, in other words, he's been transferred to team Janette, and maybe that's why he's been acting grumpy: on top of breaking up with Alice and Max, he's stuck with an old flame. Bear with me, I'm merely doing my best to humour the situation!

The gist of the job, besides the continuing case, is to establish the precise time at which the *fixed bridges* will be shut down. We have determined that all agents should be positioned in *A's world* when that happens— that's for Defense to make sure of. We must also confirm which ones of the *Firm's peons* are native to our side; Caroline and Marz will double-check. We've already been made uncertain of *the wife's* origins, so I wouldn't be surprised if we had some rogue members in the Program working for *the CEO*—I'm naturally not talking about those corrupted via associating with *Firm operatives*. As far as I'm concerned, those souls are slaves of their partners—like John.

Another item I want to see brought to fruition is identifying the location of *the CEO*. I was all fired up about finding him in the Bay Area, until Anatole showed up at the motel. The time-crossing factor is an issue that had eclipsed my rationale then. The man could be anywhere; that is, of course, if he knows about that detail. For the sake of prevention, let us just imagine that he does and that we should expect to find him somewhere between the sixties and now; or worse, between 1870 and 1900 when *the bridges* were in their last stage of operation. But that would imply he'd exist as two, which I find illogical. Rather, the way to get to *the CEO* is to get to *the wife*, which means getting to John first. Last I saw John was in Bayville, so I know he still visits with his mother in Junction Station. The sure thing is to ask mom when he next plans on coming her way. Chance, short of suggesting anything, agrees. The man is thinking—I trust he's making good use of it.

— o —

The Prof and I settle back in our old posts at both offices. As we drove along the coast, I described my life on the other side; how I came to understand the unique linearity of its evolution sine 1870, the logical trajectory of its industry, banking system, and the political landscape shaped by the two. I don't think he understood how I could have loved such a place; hence, I suggested that he give it a try by working from the house in *Bayville*. He took me on it.

In recap, three items: locating *the CEO*; arranging for all *Firm agents* to be positioned on *A's side* upon shutdown; and last, dealing with corrupt *tale-makers*.

John's mother informs me that her son never advertises his visits, and that they're generally short. His work in Buenos Aires makes it difficult, if not costly, for him to travel such a long distance. I refrain from telling her that his job doesn't prevent him from spending more time with her, to the contrary. *So, he's still up to his old tricks—he hasn't taught in the Argentines in years!* I keep it to myself. As far as the case is concerned, he and

210

Consuelo relocated to San Francisco around the time Chance moved back to Monterey. Nothing indicates he and *the wife* should be elsewhere.

The Governor didn't say when he wanted to power down the *bridges*, but I have no doubt that the sooner the better—he'll know when the time is right.

We hear from Marz that *the Firm* is planning a meeting for the 20th of December, 2000—a month from now—in *Paris* of all places! All agents have been summoned, which pretty much spells that something of utter importance is happening. It's our window of opportunity, and even if some of them remain on our side, it will be the time to strike. But I already sense something too easy in the making—it smells of a setup. The last thing *the CEO* wants to divulge is a *Firm* symposium with all of his agents in one place. It's also inconceivable that he wouldn't know of our plan to close the very system that allows him to pursue his goal of disabling the Program. Of course, him not being aware of *the erasables*, it's possible that he assumes we need the *fixed bridges* as much as he does. The fact we only disabled a fraction of them years ago, is fodder enough for him to envisage we can't afford the sacrifice of losing any more. Still, I am suspicious of the *Paris* gathering.

— o —

Only two weeks left before *the Firm's* meeting, and still no lead as to its purpose, or whether it's happening at all. My inklings send me into wild scenarios: what if *the Firm* wanted us to shut the system down, to either prove or disprove we have a replacement; or what if they too had their own means of bypassing the

211

fixed bridges? Just when I think we're ahead, we're not. They play dead for a while and then come up with a new move on the confusion game. We don't even know where they presently are at with their grand plan of disabling us. One thing for sure, they have slowed us down to a crawl.

Caroline has located the site of the summoning: a hall in the business district of *St. Denis*, not surprisingly smack in the middle of a fashion convention. It means *the wife* will be present. I believe the time has come to run into John, and so, as in all things meant to happen, his mother calls to inform me that he's on his way to Junction Station. This too could be part of a setup; sometimes one has to employ the sieve of suspicion to sort through the items that are meant to be—could be that some of them play in the bad guy's court. I ring Marz to ask how they came across the information on *Paris—One of our insiders in the Firm*, he says. *Can the source get to the origin of the leak—was he/she directly instructed to attend the meeting?* I was aware that we had embedded counter-agents, Program *defectors* acting under cover, but I'm in the dark as to their mobility across *fixed bridges*. Are those operatives going to be required to attend as well? It's actually Caroline who gets back to me: the information came from a high-ranking agent, Dantes Mansley, who leads the rogue team of *Firm sympathizers* inside the Program. How are some names always coming around when trouble knocks at the door? Mansley has all the better reasons to have a grudge against me after his forced sojourn amongst the puffin colonies of *the Faroes*. I wonder if he is counting on one of his team to make sure I get to hear about the *Paris* convention—so many convolutions, and so *A's world-like*. I cross to Chance's side of the office to give him the heads-up on what I learned from Defense. He wants to go to *Paris*, see for himself what's really going on. I approve of the call since he's working on that side, reminding him that it would be foolish to try to take the back road to *St. Denis* via Anatole's way. I knew he thought about it, because I did, but rules are rules and caution reigns. Just in case they haven't yet, *the Firm* can't stumble across the *time factor* as the result of an error of judgment! *Careful about the wife, she could be there already!* I also let him know that I plan on bumping into John tomorrow. He gets up and gives me a giant hug. We say we're sorry.

I feel a lot lighter—I guess we've made up!

— o —

John looks like Hell. I'm not saying he's old or disfigured, but his energy is all over the dark side of the map. He didn't expect me to be shopping at the same store he always stopped by before getting to his mother's house; not that it was totally coincidental, mind you. *Are you OK with me coming along to say hi to your mom; I haven't seen her in like, how long?* I lie. He doesn't even flinch; in fact, he says nothing, expresses nothing; like it's nothing more than another burden he needs to bear. He will not say, *Another time would be better!* even though I can tell he would like me to disappear. I don't force it; just, *See you there in a short while!* I load my groceries in the hydro and drive off.

John's mother knows her son well enough not to mention that she called me about his visit. It's a silent understanding between women regarding a dear one with personal troubles. We team when we judge it is the right thing to do; actually we don't even analyze, we just do.

I give them a moment to themselves before I wedge in, *How's Consuelo doing? I gather she couldn't come... Work? —Yes, preparing for a fashion show in France,* he says. I tell him it would have been nice to see her after all these years. *So, I guess, cosmetics are really catching up; who would have thought? It's like she's picked up where the industry left off in the late eighteen hundreds. Maybe someone will bring crude oil back as well!* I dare. This time, his apathy gives way to something a lot less incognisant; his blue eyes turn to the grey of anger—I have pushed a button that belongs to *the wife—*she's in there, I swear! But he recoils, or she does. Oh boy, are we in for a treat! So this is how they do it?! My shields are way up without showing—I hope. The corruption is an implant, the execrable will of trained *agents*, forcibly wedged in the psyche of each affected member. *The Firm* has hundreds of eyes within the Program! It doesn't really matter whether those agents are forever stuck in *A's world* or not, before long, they will exist on both sides simultaneously, after having created their own bridges. *The CEO* does not wish to eradicate the Program; he seeks to use it to corrupt our world! He understood the old network was finite and needed to be replaced—it was the first thing he intended on doing with the abduction of our vulnerable members, then he could concentrate on the *tale-makers* to spread the vileness of untruths. The *Paris* assembly is nothing but a trap conceived to attract Program Defense agents in revealing where we are at with our advances in alternative *bridge* design. *The Firm* always knew we had to update the old réseau at some point or another. The information given to Marz and Caroline is of ill-intent—I knew it was a setup all along, but John here and his partner showed something

I wasn't supposed to see. No fear, I shall never give them as much as an iota of detectable suspicion! As far as they observed, I didn't notice a thing!

— o —

My visit is cut short by the obligatory work stacked up at the office; an excuse as good as any other. Meeting *the wife* inside John's eyes is all the stimulation I need for now. Rushing to Chance's office only yields the vacuous sense that some danger is awaiting him in *Paris*. I must go there at once to warn him that we're about to be played. Rather than use an *erasable*, I opt for a fixed destination point with an overlay for *St. Denis*; I don't want to be seen by agents without having left traces of my travels, at least, between worlds—just a precaution.

I have been to the place during my studies in Straßburg, but it doesn't resemble anything like it. Instead of quaint neighbourhoods, I find myself amid towers and insane traffic—the cost of not preparing as we normally do when visiting the other side. All the same, I still need to find Chance. A bizarre idea strikes me: we usually seek places while crossing—never people, so what are the odds of finding someone by using their image? This time, I chose an *erasable* with a picture of Chance at the end, as the result of which we practically bump into each other on the sidewalk outside the convention center. I'm amazed at how easily that worked!

Chance guesses what's going on—he has already factored in the distinct possibility of a trap, but we're set on not going back until we get something for our efforts. We find the fashion show schedule in the lobby of the building Caroline and Marz identified for us. The only

215

clue to any *Firm* involvement is the name: *New Rise Cosmetics of Buenos Aires*, mostly because it's the only such company listed that doesn't have its headquarters in *Paris, London, New York, Rome*, or *Tokyo*.

Laterally-speaking, and as I said before, our side isn't known for its chemical makeup products and fragrances. From what I witness here, I believe what John's wife advertised back on our visit to Buenos Aires, years ago, was merchandise smuggled from here. I cannot help surmise that the loud, bright, and fast-moving stuff these shows purvey to is aimed at shortening the attention span of those already lacking in that department. But that would be the point, right? Distract and conquer! On the other hand, *the wife's* business could have been a cover all along, a decoy built on a fashion act, a walkway that serves at exhibiting the guise with shameless affront.

After some investigative work, Chance proposes that we get to the mezzanine floor that will host the *New Rise* post-show party. In spite of offering a spectacular view of the lobby, the place is hardly big or private enough for *the Firm* to conduct its dirty business; but it provides an excellent observation point for anyone monitoring ins and outs, which is how we spot *the wife* and McKenzie Henderson standing side by side. I guess *the bitch* is back! With them, comes an entourage of agents; some of which Chance recognizes from Defense files. According to him, what we have here is the core power behind *the CEO*, including Rosalia Gonzales, whom I sent to *A's Faroe Islands* from Adelaide— another who might be invested in making me pay for past deeds. Knowing we can always escape via an *erasable* if needed, we hide in the projection room, wherefrom we spy on the visiting organizers. It doesn't take us long to conclude those are operatives, not just actors—*New Rise* could be a front for a convening with a penchant for the sinister; in other words: an ambush to Program Defense. The question is, are they really that stupid? That's when Chance suggests that they probably already know we're here. *You don't mean in this room?* I ask. *Let's get the Hell out of here!* he orders.

But we can't—the space is *bridge-locked*! We make for the service door that takes us to a storage area with a supply lift at one end. Next to it, an opening onto a concrete and steel stairwell takes us down to a busy loading dock. We cross the lorry park to the safety of an *erasable*. We make it back to the office, my heart still pounding. By the look of it, Chance doesn't seem to fare any better than I do. Let's just hope *the wife* and her gang know nothing of this!

— o —

Bridge-locked is a term I never thought I would ever come across, but here it is—dangerously vivid—like an object better observed from behind safety glass. I ask Chance to explain about what made him believe we had been expected, because, frankly, I disagree. He clarifies by saying he sensed we were trapped—nothing logical. He's right, we were indeed, but I can't fathom *the CEO* wanting us to stumble across his net ahead of it being cast. *The wife* and her cohort were in the process of installing the *bridge lock*; that's what I think, and we just happened to be there when they activated it for a test run. I suspect them of seeking to attract the working core of Defense to an area contained within the wall of a *shield bell*, one which—unlike what happened in the projection

217

booth—will not allow for exit. In simpler terms: a time and space vacuum that will affect those trapped in such a way that they will carry a fractal of that *bell* with them at all times—a lot like affected Program members carry the eyes and ears of their wicked mates. I am now getting the inside view of *the Firm's viral technologies, the CEO's* investment of all his resources into nefarious sciences— all the better reasons to find him!

— o —

From the relative safety of the office, Chance and I are trying to make sense of the cluster-mess that faces us. In recap, we are being led to believe an agent symposium is about to be held in the *Paris of A's world*, a rare opportunity for us to lock the bulk of *the Firm* behind closed *bridges*. Instead, we find ourselves on the brink of redundancy, unable to identify the technology involved. I can guess about it, since in my position as the original *erasable bridge designer*, I had to contemplate the many ways of sabotaging the system; the most far-fetched of which was to render the user incapable of forming points. I never figured what could do it, but the *St. Denis* incident clearly demonstrates someone's on it. Now, I have less than two weeks to come up with an antidote, and Chance, in the meantime, must find a way to lure *the Firm* into believing they have us where they want us.

— o —

Our strategy: first, we make it look like we're biting by exposing our preparedness for the *St Denis* gathering to the *Firm's eyes and ears*; preparations which involve mobilizing Defense personnel, and plans of a secret operation reflecting our intentions to lock *the Firm* on *A's side*. In other words, all the stuff they expect of us, but without giving away the work of our counter-intelligence. That means not overdoing it!

— o —

Second: I must make my fix available to Defense without them knowing about it, because in my business we don't leave anything to chance. So far so good, but only half a dozen individuals at the department have access to *erasables*, or *fixed ones* for that matter, since teaching and training was put on freeze until further notice, years ago. I deem it the wiser to stick to the old system because, once again, I don't want to jeopardize the new. Problem is, the old is a single passenger deal, so our agents can't technically cross without a basic knowledge of *bridges*. But I trust I can fool the *fixed network* into believing an *erasable* is one of them, which would afford four of the six head operatives—the other two being Chance and I—to carry the team across.

The fix is relatively simple. It involves imprinting individual markers outside the area of *the bell* before entering it, which can be done at arrival. I immediately brief Marz and Caroline on the procedure, the two responsible for organizing the pseudo-raid.

— o —

And third: we must pretend we cannot return whence we came, in the hopes *the Firm* will finally gather to gleefully savour the fruit of their labour before moving

219

onto overtaking the Program. Chance and I will be in charge of it. That is when we strike!

The crossing will happen two days ahead of the show, which technically should give our agents plenty of time to get familiarized with the settings—just a way of going through the motions for play's sake. I believe all our ducks are in a row, as they say in *A*'s vernacular.

— o —

We find the Governor in his favourite chair upon entering the *Bayville* office. He looks elated.

Congratulations, we're ready for a shutdown of the old bridges starting 20th December! So that you know, Anatole and I have been busy keeping an eye on the CEO and the one you call 'the wife,' since the restart of the Program; their working prototype of the bell will be destroyed in the process, as it is tied to the base technology that supports the fixed bridges. The only reason why your erasable failed to function while in the booth is because it is, of your own doing, piggy-backing the old network. Of course, Chance is right, they knew where you hid; they needed you there to test the bell. What they didn't know was the fact you tried to escape through an erasable—a good thing considering the implications. They let you go to make the failure look like a common glitch—little do they know how intrinsically tied you, Janette, and the bridges are to one another. As usual, great job, both of you!

Then he's gone, except this time, I looked him straight in the eyes. I swear I saw a smile before time and space uncorked one of their favourite tricks: unexplained disappearance. One is left to wonder if it isn't just a jest of the mind... You may know what I mean.

Chance eyes me sideways, indicating he is miffed at me for being so sure of myself. I apologize—he was right about his instincts—I should never put anyone's intuitions in doubt. My way of begging for forgiveness is pretty straight forward: *When was the last time we slept together, Chance?* He doesn't try to back out of it, instead he asks in which of the two Bayvilles I want to perform the act. *Both!* I reply.

— o —

Our agents are all over *St. Denis*. If it weren't otherwise, one might think it was the Program having a conference in town. The term *agent* could be a misleader here, because we don't look like your typical operatives. For one thing—and to use an expression that has me in stitches every time I hear it—we don't pack heat! Neither do we wear anything that could betray we belong to a defense of any kind—unlike those of *the Firm* who look like they're on a mission. I'm not saying they comport themselves in the manner of enforcers, but there's a systemic demeanour to them that betrays they specialize in suspicion. As to us, we're definitely outside-the-box in our approach, which doesn't make us less organized.

We spot a multiplicity of *Firm* agents—way more than I had envisioned—something that could also be said of us, since we showed up in unexpected numbers. The place is abuzz with mobs of colourful individuals of eccentric leanings, freely acting out what I suspect society has repressed in them; for others, it is a way of life, or simply, of being theatrical for art's sake. I'm not saying this because I am a relaxed, casual observer—obviously not—but I have to maintain a façade that cannot betray

221

my apprehension. It is patent that this has a lot to do with me, the proud author of the things *the CEO* wants for himself. If I follow the rationale, by having me, Chance, and the rest of Defense removed, the *bridges* and the *tale-makers* are his. I could be wrong, but I can't explain why I would be attending this ridiculous show if I were. Anyway, Chance has joined Caroline, Marz, *One*, and my best friend *Three*—the core of Defense, that is. The convention won't start until tomorrow, but it already feels as if we were in its throes, just from the buoyancy and loud exoticism of its organizers—so many people running around! Of course, Defense is spread out for the moment, but not so for *Firm agents* in charge of setting up *New Rise Cosmetics*, although *the wife*, *the bitch*, Mansley, and Gonzales are nowhere in sight. I suspect they are putting final touches to *the bell* from an undisclosed location—a detail that may now be inconsequential. Nonetheless, I make sure to verify all the return markers are in place, even if it doesn't matter in the end. One can never make sure enough in the face of a last minute scenario, like a failed shutdown of the old system that finds us all locked in for good, say. I trust the Governor, for he's always been right, but I favour the option of an escape route over the embarrassment of none. For the moment, all the actors are readying themselves for the opening of the tabs ceremony at ten o'clock sharp.

— o —

We are in the early morning of 20th December. Head of Defense is testing *fixed bridges* out—the lane to *Bayville* is still open, and crossing over to the other Paris is a breeze. Chance and *Three* get a green light for

Monterey and Adelaide, while Caroline and Marz call it good for Straßburg, the location of their new headquarters. All is clear on the horizon, no sign of *bell activity*. Our crew is sized at seventy-seven against the hundreds of *the Firm*—not that it matters because it's not a battle, but I deem these early numbers representative of the final, critical tally. We're not overdoing it, yet our best assets are on the line. As far as *the CEO's* agents are concerned, we hope for them to all be present when it matters most: at the celebration following the defeat of Program Defense.

— o —

At exactly eleven, we are locked in—*the bell* is on! We instruct our operatives to start acting erratically, but to not overreach. We have to convey discomfort without giving away the act. I notice more of the *Firm's agents* edging closer to ours, likely monitoring behaviour. *Finesse people, finesse!* Finally, Consuelo and McKenzie Henderson, followed by Dantes Mansley and Rosalia Gonzales, appear at the top of the mezzanine's grand stairway for a quick evaluation of main lobby activity, and then briskly turn around, apparently satisfied with their observation. There isn't a doubt their agents are on each of us, three on one—most likely more—and I'm convinced *the wife's* on me, even though she no longer is visible. I get to the top of the stairs to survey what she and her people saw—it's enough, based on the ebb and flow, to get an idea of what's going on over the entire convention area. In spite of the success of their operation, it's unlikely *the Firm* will do anything until day's end when they gather for the evening party. That being said, I very much doubt they will wait the two days of the show to see us writhe. In the meantime, we need to act our parts; we assemble in small groups to then disband and reform elsewhere, as in cross-referencing our misfortunes. No panic, it's just a technicality for now; later, we'll put on a bit of the old drama, accelerate the pace to the beat of deep concern; and perhaps, near the end, we might notch up the heat to the side of frantic. That's when, technically, the snare rolls in, announcing the winner with a final rimshot, and the audience claps, whistles, and roars with pleasure—except there is no curtain call.

— o —

At five o'clock, or seventeen hour for the French, after the closing of admission, but before the crowds fully dissipate into the coldness of the winter night, the mezzanine and the lobby fill with what I gauge to be nearly six hundred attendants—a stunning number by all accounts. *The wife*, with *the bitch* by her side, calls my name into her wireless headset, asking me to come forward. I oblige, acting the part of the nobly defeated. With that, she displays me to the silent audience, which is now strictly composed of *Firm* and Program members, and begins her speech:

May I present you with Janette Trudy Smyth, designer of the tale-maker initiative, and bridge specialist at the world-renowned Program! You all have heard of the Governor, so you should know that there is no-one between him and our Janette here—she's number two! Please, a standing ovation for our special guest! [Pause for applause.] *Among you are another seventy six of the Program's agents who came here to see a special show;*

224

no, not the one the locals are already enjoying, but one of unique value to our Janette and her boss: the lockup of the Firm into this reality, by tweaking the bridges the way they did with sixty or so of our agents, nearly a decade ago. But to their chagrin, they are incapable of completing the task, because, you see, they can no longer operate these bridges—they have been shut out of them with never a chance to return to their world and their darling program! Their entire defense team is in this very hall, useless, trapped forever in a city that will show them no mercy! Before long, and we'll make sure of it, they will be walking the streets, resourceless, defenseless, and utterly defeated, while we take over their life's work, their labour of love, and return their precious world to where it belongs: this ONE—OURS; until the two become indistinguishable from each other. My only regret is that our Janette will be long gone before she can enjoy the results of what she started—so sad! Everyone, say 'Poor Janette'! The *Firm's* roused collective ego screams, *POOR JANETTE!!!* then they all vanish. Left are Program Defense, including its counter-agents, and *the wife* who stares fixedly at the sudden, silent emptiness.

— o

According to the Governor, the way system-shutdown works, each active user from *A's side*—regardless of the time and place of their last travel, or whether they crossed to our side or not—returns to the initial point of their first-ever use of the system; a function implemented at the reopening of the *bridge network* in the early sixties. Consequently, *the Firm* found its agents scattered around the globe without knowledge

225

of the others' whereabouts, and no means of transport other than conventional ways. Additionally, their Program partners—the unfortunate corrupted souls—came free, because *the CEO's* entire technology was borrowed from the *bridge* platform, an energy source proprietary to the Program and the force behind *the erasables*. He simply happened to stumble upon that knowledge, courtesy Consuelo de Aranjuez, whilst trapped inside all those years—the one single event that likely wasn't meant to be! Mind you, we don't know to this day how he got in there in the first place. In the meantime, he's still at large and *the wife* miraculously vanished—finally proving she is from our world—while John is nowhere to be seen. My take is that those are separate issues. Wherever John ends up being, I hope it's a good place, for I am sure he could use the break.

——— o ———

27 – IN-BETWEEN YEARS

When Chance and I returned to Bayville from the show in *St. Denis*, we made a pact of never again straying too far from each other. It was over eighteen years ago and we stuck to it!

Though we had won a decisive battle against the Firm, much was still to be done in terms of rehabilitating the victims of agent abduction, locating the CEO and the wife, tracing the work of corrupt tale-makers scattered in *A's world*, and of course, of teaching advanced bridge-building to old and new students alike, among the many tasks an overseer faces on a daily basis. It is why I shall return to that era to resume with my story. But first, I want to tell about *A*.

—— o ——

In 2004, something extraordinary happened. *A*, who had gone through years of substantial soul-searching, appeared in one of my dreams. As you know, since the mid-eighties, I had carried the discomforting feeling of being short on space in my given mental and emotional environment, so *A*, who was naked by the side of my own nakedness, informed me that my story was made of two parts: the first, starting in this very present of 2019, and the other, beginning in the eighties, which is the one that took Chance and I to the *St. Denis* fashion show. It made little sense since I clearly remembered writing about my early life, plus my body wanted him more than my mind was willing to accept alien information, but I managed to ask him where I could find the writing of that first story. *It's with you,* he said, *but I promise it will be written one day, should you not find it within yourself.* I am almost certain we made love before we both vanished from the realm of consciousness.

I believe *A* actually said that my first story was the item crowding my space, like another me among the clutter of the self, and that there had been two cohabiting versions of my present, one in the making, and the other which already had happened. But what does one expect from dreams?! From my standpoint at the time, it meant that two Janettes shared a space, and that, eventually, they would have to become one again. Deep down, it made a lot of sense, since it was in character for me to want to change the past if something unimaginable were to happen in my present. It didn't take me long to figure out what that unimaginable might have been—that was what convinced me of *A's* words. That day, I understood why it was all the more important to revive the case and go after the CEO and the wife. I called Chance.

— o —

After *St. Denis*, a class on the fixed system of bridges started its first steps at the Program. It was about time that we introduced to advanced students one of the fundamentals of our history. We kept some of the details out of it, but the incident of 1870 and the separation of the two worlds became known to all. Bridge-building wasn't to be implemented until it was clear it lined up with the evolution of what is better known today as the New Program, started a few years before I joined First Generation. With the closure of the old system and the defeat of the Firm, we, meaning the faculty, reopened full admission into Chapters, as well as created new ones. Marz and Caroline assigned the resources of Defense to the rehabilitation and retraining of the corrupted souls, but most often, to their transfer to a special facility in Hobart, Tasmania, where they would spend the rest of their lives under the care of specifically trained personnel. It's sad, but yet, they suffered the consequences of weaknesses the Program offered to alleviate, but to which they failed to respond. We now have a way of sifting through the admission process in order to eliminate the chance of it to ever happen again.

We didn't think, at the level of the Overseers, or First Generation, as we are often referred to, that the disappearance of the CEO and his second-in-command, Consuelo de Aranjuez, was of any concern—the way we saw it, a firm without a staff was a non-entity. I'm not saying that Chance and I let go of Defense without a modicum of apprehension, but resources were much needed in other areas; thus, the department was retired. During that time, I worked heavily on defining the deep layers of bridge-building, a task that took me into astounding possibilities. Let me keep it simple by saying that the erasables are capable of opening onto many worlds—not just the two—across an infinity of time points. That area of experimental research kept the picture of the wife vivid in my mind, as she stood alone at the top of the mezzanine's grand stairs, looking into the nothingness of the Firm. But more importantly, she left with the secret of how she was able to elude us.

The process of fixing the damage caused by the corrupted tale-makers, took Chance and I into *A's reality* on a tour of writers, publishers, and libraries, with the intention of convincing them to edit irregularities or remove the works. But the job implied the use of such draconian measures, that, in the end, we decided that the damage was part of the cost of having taken too much time to force the Firm out. As it so happened, the harm was so consistent with everyday occurrences that it passed for another item of common corruption—invisible, and a lot less potent than the messages that carried hope.

— o —

The day following the *St. Denis* show was the last I saw of the Governor, at least, the way I was used to knowing him: tall, stately, vibrant, and very old-school. He is around, but more in essence than in the flesh; although one could say he never was a physical being. I always thought of him as a guardian, as opposed to a teacher. Technically, he was the professor who tutored me to become one myself, but he never showed up for class, deeming, rather, that all the knowledge I needed was locked within me, and that the true training was in my ability to recognize the intrinsic relationship that existed between teacher and student.

The Governor's strongest asset is to always know the exact time at which one's work is done and when one's qualities are at their most receptive to validation. To say that he practically lives within us is to understand the true nature of his mission.

— o —

The years between the show and my dream with *A* constituted, short of better words, a stage from which to

230

evaluate the New Program. Much was accomplished, yet there was a sense of routine to the workday that lacked the spontaneity of the early years. I think we were drained of momentum by the ominous presence of the Firm and the continuous dosage of *A's world* energy spread around by the corrupted souls. We were in repair mode and not quite ready to build our next platform. It is why my story isn't dedicating much to that period. Chance was in Monterey most of the time, but we arranged to see each other regularly for a mix of work and pleasure. When time permitted, we took the mighty hydro or Little Honda on trips to the country, or to trailheads for occasional hikes in the coastal mountains. Some marvel that I still use these two autos to this day. I get attached to few things, but when I do, they become part of me, and I tend to treat them like I do my own body: with loving care. *That's why you girls look so good!* Chance often humoured and still does. Bless his sweet soul!

—— o ——

28 – CONSUELO DE ARANJUEZ

Chance showed up immediately following my call. Just like me, he felt the time had come to get back to where we had left off. He never fully agreed with the precocious retirement of Defense and the way precious logistic assets, such as Caroline and Marz's departments, had been reduced to the job of reorienting the corrupted souls. For me, the disappearance of Consuelo de Aranjuez always sat in the background, its shadow spreading in places I could no longer see; I knew it was there, but its access was forbidden to me in ways I cannot recount. It was a paralysis of sort at the mental level, while a voice, deep within, frantically sought to warn me. It took *A* to wake me to it—the alarm that pulled me out of my spell.

That deep, urgent churning was merely perceived as a nameless nagging feeling, as in the procrastinated items that keep on falling to the bottom of the list, because more important ones bully their way to the top; except that me and the rest of First Generation were the ones setting the order of importance, which was more cosmetic than it was integral to the deep workings of the Program. A crude analogy, using the passenger flying machines of *A's world*, would be in keeping on polishing the skin ahead of a crash caused by structural failure as the result of negligence. Apathy in the face of danger was likely what happened there. Again, the looming influence of the work of the Firm was slow to dissipate. It took us years to realize how deep that energy had run, in spite of damage control. It would have been a matter of weeks for it to overtake the Program, had we not shut out its agents on that pivotal winter day in *Paris*. It was quite clever on the part of the CEO to bridge the gap between his team and our unsuspecting members for the transfer of darkness into our world, while our corrupted tale-makers sent poison-laced prose back the other way, with the aim of blackening the literary mind and silencing the voice of hope. He understood the nature of sympathetic points quite well, and the power capable of traveling between them; something against which we were ill-prepared to take action, since the concept was alien to us. But it made me aware that similar potential in the erasables could be harnessed for the pursuit of much nobler and useful causes, such as the healing of worlds. In other words, that energy—part of the universal makeup—was ready to be tapped to serve the layers of communication, like it had served us with the bridges. After all, it had served nature from the beginning, for it is what connects all. The dominant human trait, isolationism, pushed away the notion of oneness-with-all from the onset; and thus, the mind never saw what was readily available. Instead, it stole—short of a better word—what it deemed belonged to it, calling it invention. The Program was created to offset that imbalance, by those who called themselves the Governors. But I think I have said enough on the topic of history for now.

— o —

Chance and I split the job in the middle, with him taking on the CEO, and me, Consuelo. We knew they were both in our world, but I suspected the wife was able to cross over, for she seemed to have something no-one else in the Firm possessed: the ability to manœuvre in the absence of fixed bridges. I undoubtedly would have moved a lot sooner, had I allowed myself to imagine she possessed knowledge of the erasables. Perhaps, it was sheer hubristic drive that blocked me from contemplating the possibility someone else was on the same path as I was—or worse—that I, or Chance, or anyone of the six with the clearance to build bridges, had been negligent enough to be spied on by the wife while crossing. I originally explained that the nature of traveling that way didn't lend itself to observation, but we are talking about Consuelo de Aranjuez, the CEO's right hand, hence a different set of rules.

— o —

By splitting the pie, I, of course, meant that we each had a part in locating the two. I personally believed the CEO was going to be a lot easier to find than the wife. I based that feeling on the fact that he was beyond old, and that his drive for retaliation against the 1870 historical interference by the Program was losing steam. One with a different perspective might also have said that he had never been located, that his identity was questionable, and that, in all likeliness, he didn't even exist. I understood the logic, but I viscerally felt him—to me, he had never ceased being around. The strangest thing—and I had absolutely no idea where it came from—was this particular draw to the Oakland hills, as if a beacon had been emitting a signal advertising his presence. I didn't see the point of wasting time on research, hence why I asked Chance to give the area a try. After all, Defense had come up empty after years of tracking agents, so an intuition was the best we had for a head start. I sensed he was agreeable with my request when he said, *Two meshing gears are better than one spinning free!* It takes a guy to come up with something like that, but I got the idea. He asked to return to Monterey first to put order to his thoughts, before driving to Oakland and get on with it. I obliged on the condition we spend the night together. On times like those, love-making was intimately tied to life—like breathing—moments free of a yesterday and a tomorrow—the present undisturbed. We kissed goodbye in the early morning. I cried.

— o —

The way I located Consuelo was fairly straight forward, although it had its complications. I used her image the same way I did Chance's when I needed to find him in *Paris*, but I couldn't afford to bump into her like with the Prof on that occasion. So, I had to fine-tune my design. I failed miserably for days on end building that safe bridge, until I discovered a way to incorporate variable distances into the image. For example, I first dialed her up while calling *any city*; Straßburg flashed in my mind but the bridge didn't take me there, for that, I would have had to dial in that location. But it made perfect sense. Next, I tuned to the Straßburg Chapter, since I had a permanent room there, as it was the case with the other six at First Generation, who, if I haven't already made mention of it, were now all part of the bridge-builder league. I'm speaking mostly for *Two*, *Four*, and *Five*, who weren't with Defense. Remember, I'm *Seven*, Chance is *Six*, and *One* and *Three*, my married friends from Adelaide, comprise the rest. Just making sure we're on the same page! Anyway, I materialized in my room at the Chapter, and rather than stay on the wife, I relaxed my pace to think things over. I doubted she was going to stay idle, so figuring out a means to not lose her the minute she was found was paramount—hence how I arrived at the concept of the tracking bridge: a movable version capable of keeping a steady distance. I always loved it when field work served double duty!

— o —

Indeed, Consuelo de Aranjuez moved! Before I could search the city, she was already gone—but I stayed. There was no redeeming element in losing my concentration by chasing a banshee all over the world— some of it felt like a diversion anyway. And why did I feel that way? Simply because I didn't think she was hiding as much as she had been spying all these years. So, the best way to know was to wait for her return. I was right; she was back in Straßburg within days, which comically brought me to size the situation as two cats seeing each other as mice. But I had my reasons, so what were hers? It was my first case outing in years; she had no idea what I had done in the meantime—what I had accomplished in bridge design—and since I utilized a proprietary system for tapping energy, she couldn't have matched my research without the Firm behind her. What she could have done on the other hand, was develop unique ways to go around and channel information, with the aim of recruiting agents in order to finish what she'd started. The thought wasn't new; it existed dormant as part of the procrastination I mentioned earlier: that sense of apathy that froze me in my thinking tracks. I could have hated myself for it if I hadn't known any better, so rather than lamenting, I doubled down on my determination to end the charade once and for all. It was no longer relevant to locate the wife, since she was always going to be within close range, hoping for a window into my advances in bridge-building. Although by staying close to her, I took the chance of exposing my ways of travel; it was how I figured out she was also capable or tracking me, which revealed a sympathetic connection between her bridges and mine—they communicated with each other. It was something I had grossly overlooked, and consequently, Consuelo de Aranjuez must have known I had recently been on her tail, hence why she chose to be in Straßburg where she wanted me most. But then, instead of following her, I stayed put. I believe it confused her. Could I have been in town for reasons other than her? At that point, I was the cat and she the mouse, but I didn't intend on letting her know that.

Technology-wise, I deemed she possessed a few elements useful in helping her manœuver her way around, but with limitations. It was why she sought what I had, and why it became essential for me to strengthen my shields, because erasability was no longer enough.

— o —

It was my understanding that Consuelo de Aranjuez had a team working under her command, but I didn't fathom any of them came from the other side. It led me to trust that they lacked the motivation of the Firm, and that their usefulness was strictly under a false cover. Yes, they certainly spied on us, but the reasons were disparate. Again, all speculations on my part were the

237

results of an analysis of possibilities; I had no intention of going down Delusion Alley. I think I made it clear, so far, that I favoured working my way from the back door to the front. It was not a novel idea by any stretch of the imagination, but rather than subtracting from evidence, I did it from possibilities, which gave me a lot more latitude to be creative with the process. That being said, I was not in the habit of going after the intangible—why I stayed behind in Straßburg.

When the wife returned, we found ourselves in the position of watching each other, with the difference that I knew her game, while she could only guess mine. In the process of it happening, I reflected on the nature of her present connection with the CEO: were they working together, or had she gone solo? It was of great importance in sussing the larger picture: were we back in the pre-days of the fashion show, or were we playing a different game altogether? If so, who in the world was Consuelo de Aranjuez? I had found it easy to slap a name on the CEO, as hypothetical as that might have been, but the wife's mystery had never ceased to deepen. With that, I also started thinking about John and why he hadn't resurfaced after all these years...

— o —

A shield of invisibility was nothing more than a switch in the off position. The bridge could no longer communicate with others, and since it also self-erased, my ways of travel exponentially increased in stealth. But if it cut visibility in one direction, it left it open in the other—a one-way glass, so to speak. But yet, the shield could keep the last image active if I chose—let's say, I would be having dinner with my parents in Bayville, while the wife thought I was in Straßburg. I was at a point with the erasables where the possibilities had become endless—by then, the system was second-nature, like a skin. The energy that drove them was the one that kept me ageless; me, and all of those who had been in direct contact with it, namely Defense and First Generation. It went without saying that Consuelo de Aranjuez had also benefited from it, for, by most standards, she was ancient. That year, 2004, was an extremely pivotal time in terms of my personal growth and metamorphosis. I was fifty, yet I felt energized, young in a way that my experience no longer carried the ages. I didn't desire to live forever, but I sensed the winds of history as if they were blowing along paths I had already traveled—an utterly odd feeling of timelessness was taking hold.

— o —

I returned to Straßburg to resume with my watch. I suspected the wife was about to do something reckless, something desperate. I couldn't help but sense she had surmised that I was in town for matters that had nothing to do with her, an insult borne of dangerous reasoning, and an indication she had lost her compass. She walked straight into my open room, expecting me there, but I stood in the dorm at the end of the hall, spying from behind the peephole. She came out, brandishing a firearm. By the look of it, if she couldn't get what she sought, she was going to make sure I would never enjoy the fruit of my work; in other words, she wanted me dead. But I had a hold on her; I saw her, and she could no longer see me, which explained her fury. She vanished before my eyes, but I could care less where she went—she would be of no consequence until I further refined my bridge onto her. In the meantime, I sensed Chance needed my help with his assignment, and so, in typical fashion, we bumped into each other in Oakland.

— o —

The CEO was old—very old. It was clear he and Consuelo de Aranjuez hadn't been partners in years. He looked frail in the wheelchair provided by the retirement home. His name was indeed John Rockefeller; I was right about that. But he, of course, wasn't the magnate of *A's world*. One thing to his credit: he was aware of the 1870's bit of modification that robbed him of his fortune; but then again, he learnt of it later, while locked inside the fixed bridge system from which he was also able to buy time. After all, without it, he would have been a hundred and sixty-five—the end was obscenely overdue.

John had found his name in the main library register. He was an avid reader, a member for the last nine years. He had sought the services of the home two years prior, and since then, we were told he never had a visit. He was alone at a table, playing with small figures neither of us cared to make sense of. He looked up; unfazed by the sight of two individuals he once considered prime targets of the Firm's ill will. Rather the opposite, he was glad we came, as if he had been waiting.

He knew our names, although he kept his focus on me, practically ignoring Chance. He didn't feel the need to apologize any more than I wanted him to—we were well beyond past resentments and the mundanity of making up. Of the wife, much was said in the form of disdain pointed at her stealth and ruthlessness. He had met her before the closure of the bridges. It was she who informed him about the US/France treaty and what he had lost in the process. She poisoned his mind with promises of retribution for what the Program had done to him, having no idea, at the time, what the Program even was, but her story was compelling and he fell for it. In the end, she convinced him to follow her across the bridge to witness his double's good fortune, but instead, he ended up being left in the system—trapped. De Aranjuez contacted him as soon as he got out, in early 1961. In spite of his initial distrust, they joined forces to steadfastly built wealth and contacts, until they found themselves in position to launch the Firm, but it was her idea all along. In the end, he realized she had used him as a façade—he was the CEO of a firm with no raison d'être. Save for the dispensation of a few items of cosmetics smuggled from the other side, there was no legitimate business. She used him because he had the necessary savvy for raising fast money when she needed it—a talent that also served him well in building a private fortune in entertainment. He had no idea what the other world looked like; in fact, he never cared. But, had it not been for Consuelo de Aranjuez's intermittent company while trapped in the system, he would have gone insane by the time he was let out. In spite of the selfishness of her act, it contributed to keeping him oriented through his predicament—for that, he was grateful. At the peak of their relationship, he developed an interest in what she did—it was how he became aware I was the prized item, alongside the Governor and the rest of First Generation. The CEO confirmed that de Aranjuez wanted full control of the Program and the bridges, but from his perspective, he sensed that there were two scenarios in play—it remained undetermined whether she would win or lose. "Maybe both," he said. The matter-of-factness of that statement rang deep within me. Yes, there was the part in which she had already won; it was in the winds of the paths already traveled, but those winds belonged to a future that was no longer—I had taken it with me. All that was left was a *now* where Chance and I stood facing a very old man who was never meant to be among us, the odd piece that fell off the stack of adjusted history for no other purpose than showing that balance had been disturbed. But time had taken care of it. The CEO was about to leave, and with him, the reasons for returning a stolen reality to the fold. Perhaps, what was not meant to be had found its place after all. Old man John Rockefeller was ready—he had no regrets. We understood then what the wife had done to him: even though he had never been on the other side, he had served as the portal through which much darkness had traveled from it. By the time her last agent had found her eyes in the Program, she was done with him. Chance and I had heard enough.

— o —

In the case of Consuelo de Aranjuez, knowing of her whereabouts didn't necessarily dictate how to proceed. Even though I understood madness had taken hold of her and that she was dangerous, I could find neither the reason nor the method to neutralize her. I couldn't take away a tool that was borne of the very energy that connected all living things; that tool, those bridges belonged to her—she had earned them. Even though she desired to take mine away from me, retaliation wasn't part of the language we spoke, and neither was *A's* version of right and wrong. We, at the Program, sought to comprehend and validate. I strived to understand what made her tick, what made her so angry to the point of needing to create a persona to serve that anger. I wanted to know where she came from, if she was one of the early Overseers, and what it was about 1870 that had given her reason to corrupt a multi-millennial organization. I needed to know wherefrom she drew her powers. Had she advanced to them via special aptitudes and training, or did she feed on misappropriated Program energy? In other words, I needed to unravel the mystery of her person before I could actually fight her. Although *fight* wasn't the word of choice—*contend with*, perhaps.

I realized it would take years before I got there. Surely, it was reckless to wait, but there was no way around choosing my battle. It was me she wanted, never mind the Program, and I was only willing to confront her after having sorted out what made her—her strengths and weaknesses.

— o —

Chance and I closed the Firm case. With the CEO gone and only one loose cannon left in a concurrent system of bridges, we faced an oddity at best. My attempts to connect with the Governor for his knowledge on Consuelo de Aranjuez were met with an absence that discomforted me deeply. If he judged that I had to figure it out for myself, it meant there was still a lesson to be learnt before the time came to face the wife; although it reassured me about my choice of exercising caution.

We originally had established that de Aranjuez was born in the years between the US/French alliance and the time of the bridge shutdown in 1900, and that her youthfulness was due to having spent sixty or so years locked in the system. But another theory arose from our meeting with John Rockefeller at the nursing home: she had only been inside intermittently, which signified she already possessed an intimate knowledge of it and had means of access despite its closure. She preceded me as a bridge-builder by decades and was on her way to develop her own version of the erasables when something came down. She might even have been the reason why the Governor closed the fixed bridges in the first place. I sensed that by doing so, he had been buying time, the time necessary to find the one to replace her. For that, he would have had to know I would eventually apply to the New Program. Well, thinking of it, I never applied; he asked me in, like the other six of First Generation—me being the last, with Chance ahead of me.

As usual, I used my trusted method of creating plausible scenarios and eliminating what didn't fit as I moved along the evidence. It was clear that the emergence of my world through the actions of 1870 did not agree with Consuelo; hence she couldn't have been born after that date, as it was first speculated. She most likely was in the Old Program, at about the same level I was when I first came across the erasables, which was—perhaps not so coincidentally—around the time of that party in San Francisco, at the art gallery, when I first met her through John—an introduction I can't forget due to the way she so intensely scrutinized me. In retrospect, she had been after me all along, which explained why she chose John as her slave-mate. But regardless of her origin, or what she possessed in terms of bridge know-how, the question remained: why did she wish to erase my world? Maybe the answer resided in the loss of her place of power because of it, and I was born in it. But she still had *A's reality*; surely, she was not deprived of her powers there; but then again, why was she left standing at the top of the mezzanine stairs, in *St. Denis*, when all of her agents were sent away? Likely, she belonged to both as I did, unless she was from another world altogether.

The thought awoke me to yet another aspect of bridge-building, which to that point, I had refused to contemplate: dimensionality in the form of infinite variations on history. That was a lot more than I had bargained for; my mind was caught in a storm that sought to blow me off-course. As much as I was willing to explore lateral thinking, I had my limits. I suddenly felt exhausted. It was time for Chance and I to take off for the wilderness, something we promised to do but rarely acted on. We were grossly overdue for a proper camping trip, away from all things Program.

— o —

We indeed took off for two weeks in the mountains of *A's world*. The protected land there emitted a song that told of a deeper story than that of our forests; it had urgency in it, contrast, dynamics—a resonance that agreed with where we were at level-wise. By no means were we slacking on the urgency of defining the Consuelo de Aranjuez character; rather, the back of the beat, if I may say, was aimed at providing perspective. Chance and I finally concluded that the wife simply originated from the pre-split era—the idea of yet another world being too far-fetched in spite of its exoticism. It didn't mean that I wasn't going to explore the depths of bridge technology, but I needed to simplify, extract by reduction. Yes, I did indeed say that I wanted to stay away from the matters of the Program while we were away, so we did exactly that: enjoy the company of species that lived within the sanctity of refuges created by those who knew their place in the universe—not an easy task when nobility was deemed a weakness. There wasn't a doubt the wilderness of *A's world* had shrunk to critical levels, but one wouldn't have known from inside it; it was just as majestic as ours when you ignored the forces that pushed against it. Chance and I bonded with it, made love to it, and let ourselves be cocooned by it; the healing going both ways, big and small. We returned to the Program reenergized and feeling deliciously wholesome.

— o —

One major inconsistency emerged from the theory Consuelo de Aranjuez was born before 1870. Just like the CEO, she would have existed in both realities, and thus irrevocably been prevented from traveling between worlds. But then, the same could have been said of the Governor, though we pretty much knew he originated from an earlier time period—same as Anatole the poet. I was left to consider the wife was one of them—that she did not actually exist in our time. It was all so confusing!

— o —

For the moment, I was safe as long as I stayed a step ahead of Consuelo de Aranjuez. Any rational mind would have acknowledged that it was a matter of time before the tables turned—I had to make a move quickly.

246

It was well observed that preys were all the more dangerous when they felt hunted; there wasn't a doubt the wife had found herself in that position. Even though she could no longer find me with the help of her bridges, there was always the old-fashioned way of locating one's enemies—but again, I had the means to check on her, which I did at increasingly tight intervals. She had remained in Straßburg since the dorm incident, but that could easily have been a decoy, if she had, just as I did, found a way to conceal her whereabouts. But I preferred to eliminate that thought, since my intuitions did not warn me of such a scenario. Her presence in Straßburg simply signified she was stationed there, near the stately structure that had housed the Old Program, and which had been repossessed by the Governor to serve as headquarters of the new one. It was where I was meant to find her and face her wrath.

Chance accompanied me back to my room at the Chapter. The bridge informed us Consuelo de Aranjuez was on campus, more precisely, in the vicinity of the Governor's office. I had the odd feeling something was up that didn't bode well, making it official it was time for the inevitable tête à tête. I ordered Chance to stay behind and to only intervene if I wasn't back within fifteen minutes. I didn't bother going through the dean's office to get to the Gov's den. It was dark inside, with only a slit between the heavy curtains to allow for a beam of daylight to cut the space in halves. I stood on one side while the wife stood on the other, by the chair behind the desk. She barely flinched, although a slight tremor in her aura betrayed that she hadn't been expecting me quite yet. I switched on the lights; the Governor was bent over like a broken reed, most assuredly dead. Consuelo sized me up like one does a thing that has been in the way for too long, ready for the final removal. I had no fear; it had been my destiny all along, the moment that was meant to be: the facing of an ancient Governess gone rogue, whose place, as she likely saw it, I had usurped. Whatever powers she possessed were below my troubles. Certainly, a woman who resorted to the use of a firearm couldn't have many left. As she pointed the weapon at my head and wished me luck in Hell, I superimposed her face over an image of a vacuous space of absolute blackness intent on representing her final destination, a special bridge I painstakingly designed in preparation of that inevitable encounter. Just as she pulled the trigger, her body assumed a momentary tilt that sent the bullet grossly off-target. Her eyes turned the pale grey of rage, or fear, or whatever Consuelo de Aranjuez felt when her life was no longer within her reach. I made sure to lock my gaze to hers, so that her last memory of me could never be erased. Then, with a final shudder of her image, she was gone.

— o —

The Governor didn't make it, but I knew it was meant to be—he lived on in whatever form or capacity, just like Consuelo de Aranjuez would in the absence of a physical world—you simply couldn't kill an eternal soul. The tall man was recalled by time, soon gone from his chair—no trace of his existence in this present of mine would ever be found. Like he was never there to greet me to the Program, or at my office when he took me across the bridge to *A's world*, into a house he once owned in *Bayville*, directly across mine, the same place painted a different colour. But some memories can't be erased.

Chance joined me—the fifteen minutes had elapsed. We stood there for a while, looking around the empty office for no clues in particular—it was just time to turn the page.

I rang the small bell that let the dean know someone was coming out—the swing-door opened. The man barely looked at us when he said, *Have a good day, Ms. Smyth!*

— o —

Yes, it wasn't totally unexpected. After all, I had been in the Program long enough to be aware this would happen one day—you simply didn't come to the point at which there was nothing between you and the Governor, or, as the wife once insinuated by calling me number two, without becoming the Governor yourself. And because, my story happened, as it still does, in the relative quality of time and space, we entered the Governor's office via a bridge in early 2005 to exit through the door in 2012.

What happened to the time in between? Well, I could take you there, like I did when I returned to the eighties to fix the past, but it was a lot of the same; plus, I promised *A* that I would keep the story to roughly two hundred and fifty pages. But before we come to an end, there are a few more things that must be said.

— o —

For one, the story of the Governor and Consuelo de Aranjuez is long and complex. Let me just say that these two were, or rather are, the parts of an inseparable whole that foresaw different uses of the Program to the

249

pursuit of uniquely different ends. The gist of my story rests within one basic principle: for *A's world* to survive, another had to be created to offset the evils that had taken hold by the time the Prussian War rose in the distance. It would be unfair to say the wife was the sole brewer of such ills, but let's assume that she had an invested interest in seeing that version of reality realize its full potential. As it was, the Governor saw otherwise. He also saw that for the Program to survive, he and Consuelo de Aranjuez had to be reclaimed by the very forces that had put them in my time in the first place, forces that belonged to another era, one that saw the rise of the temples from the standpoint of a present facing futures in all of their possible manifestations. As I said, it's a long story that I shall leave to another tale-maker to tell. As to me, well, it was of crucial importance that I should grow up in the *new world*, fundamentally free of the divide that separates me from *A's side*, and the one between the Gov and the wife; plus the Program needed a world unifier in the form of a new Governor—it just so happened that it was meant to be Seven all along.

—— o ——

29 – JOHN'S FATE

John resurfaced in late 2012. Eight years had passed since the dismissing of the wife, and twelve since the Firm was defeated. We met again at an art show in Bayville. He looked aged and a bit disheveled, but he was healthier than I had expected him to be. Unlike the other corrupted souls that went through the various rehabilitation sessions designed to reincorporate them in the New Program, or allow them to live under overseer care in Hobart, John opted for soul-searching without help instead. But I saw an issue in it: he couldn't be out of the system with the kind of knowledge he possessed, plus, he was also a tale-maker using proprietary methods for aims that could easily have been dubious. He also was Consuelo de Aranjuez's husband, and for the longest time, her eyes and ears in the Program, so I had good reasons to keep a watch on him.

When he asked how the Governor was doing, I just said *fine*—he didn't need to know anything more about it. In other words, I did not trust him. But that didn't prevent me in turn from asking if he had any intention of reapplying, for he was in a legitimate position to do so. It was of course a set-up—I absolutely had to know where he stood. He said he needed to think about it. He had a month to get back to me with an answer—that was my ultimatum!

As anticipated, he returned to me exactly a month later with a positive response; he wanted back in the Program as a professor in tale-making. I accepted, but under the condition he submitted himself to deep examination for potential traces of corruption, to which he agreed. During that time, he and I met on regular intervals to discuss the pertinent details of his relationship with his wife, the mastermind behind the Firm. He didn't like talking about her, and I didn't like him not to, but he was in no place to choose, pleasant or not. He shared to a point, but I soon established he was incapable of giving me what I wanted: how she ended up being inside him. I guessed he didn't possess the knowledge, or wasn't permitted to tell, from which I concluded the wife was still in there—somehow. Unlike the first version of my story in which we met at the seafood place, and during which I wasted precious time trying to figure out what was wrong with him, I wasn't going to allow him—or her—to walk me in circles. I was the Governor—anything but firmness was unthinkable.

So, as far as I understood, John was gone, and Consuelo de Aranjuez was back at her old tricks, although with serious limitations. But before things could fester into yet another situation, I decided to nip the problem in the bud; I opted for the one solution that had been used in neither the Old Program nor the new one: complete deconditioning, even if it meant John would remain a vegetable for the rest of his useful life. Caroline and Marz took care of it. John had moved on a long time ago, and all I was left with were memories of our time together in the late nineteen-sixties, memories of play amid the hippie camps of Junction Station.

— o —

Today, in the company of Chance, I am looking at the ocean from the long beach of San Francisco. We just returned from a trip we took down to Monterey in the classic hydro. We chose once again to book a room at the old and faithful motel we've been using for decades. One last time, before I fully let him go, I briefly think of John and of his love for his perpetual-motion riding machine, the one he took me in when we met for fish and lazy strolls to the Ferris wheel at the end of the boardwalk. But that belongs to another story that fares poorly for the New Program, this world, and *A's*; one I'm glad will never be told.

Before we part, I must say that I love Chance with all my heart—we're blessed with the gift of time to probe wherever deep that love will take us. But *A* will forever be with me, for he is me, the *me* I've never been able to hide from; a character without whom I simply couldn't exist.

With love,
Janette Trudy Smyth, 27th May 2019

OTHER WORKS
BY THE AUTHOR

— The Disappearance of Olaf Swyndle
(An Improbable Emergence Volume 1)
© 2016

— The Hektor Dilemma
(An Improbable Emergence Volume 2)
© 2016

— Ma-l's Grand Gathering
(An Improbable Emergence Volume 3)
© 2017

— Convergence of the Realms
(An Improbable Emergence Volume 4)
© 2017

— Escape from Inconsequence   © 2018

— Reyes & Leeds   © 2018

—Nine Amber Pieces   © 2019

—A Life Given, a Life Taken   © 2020